JENNIFER KILLICK

PROJECT Z

DREAD WOOD

FRIGHT BITE

KU-225-126

Farshore

CHAPTER ONE

A TRAGIC START

'What. The. Heck. Is. That?' Colette says, as the sound of a horn honking like a deranged goat makes everyone within a hundred-metre radius stare in the direction of the school car park. We're standing outside Dread Wood High in the fading light, looking fresh in the clothes we just changed into, our uniforms squashed in our backpacks.

It's 4 p.m. on a Thursday, so most of the

students have gone home, but there are still some hangers-on: the after-school club attenders and the detention slackers. I'd been feeling pleased that for once I wasn't one of the detention slackers, but the smugness is fading fast when I see what's driving up the path.

'Oh god.' Hallie looks up from her phone. 'Please tell me that isn't our ride.'

But as the school minibus pulls up to where we're waiting, it becomes clear that, tragically, it *is* our ride.

'Anyone for a road trip?' Mr C grins at us out of the open window. 'I even pimped our wheels – look!'

We turn to where he's pointing and see that he's stuck a hand-painted banner on the side of the bus, underneath the windows from which our faces will be fully visible when we're inside. It says: *HAVE A PENG BIRTHDAY!*

'I'm sorry I couldn't include your name on the banner, Colette, for safeguarding reasons,' Mr Canton says. 'But I wanted to make it special.'

'That's honestly totally fine.' Colette's cheeks are bubblegum pink and she looks like she'd rather be anywhere than here. If one of the Latchitts' trapdoor spiders was to burst out of the gravel and drag her underground, she'd probably thank it and welcome a doom less excruciating than a birthday trip in the school minibus.

'Sir, when you said you'd got us a "sick vehicle", I thought you meant a limo. Or a Humvee with blacked-out windows,' Gus says.

Colette's mum leans over from the passenger seat. 'Well, he got you Betty, which I'm sure you'll agree is even better. Come on, get in.'

'Betty *is* an excellent name.' Gus nods, patting the minibus like it's a very good dog.

'Come on, let's get this over with,' Naira sighs, pulling on the handle and sliding the door open, like she's no stranger to using this method of transportation.

'Sliding that door like a pro.' I raise an eyebrow at her.

'Not my first rodeo,' she says, climbing on board and scooching along one of the rows of seats to the opposite end.

'Dibs the back row,' Hallie says, pushing past the rest of us and jumping inside. 'I can't believe you didn't take it, Naira.' She runs to the rear and drapes herself across three of the fake-leather-covered seats. 'You had an open goal right there.'

'A Year Seven kid vommed there a couple of weeks ago, on our way to a chess tournament,' Naira says. 'Just so you know.'

Hallie sausage rolls off the seat and on to the floor while the rest of us laugh. 'Gross,' she says, and takes the row behind Naira instead.

'Don't worry, it's been thoroughly sanitised!' Mr C smiles over his shoulder as Gus hops on and slides along the seats so he's next to Naira.

'There are eleven empty seats on this minibus, so why are you squishing up next to me?' Naira says, although she doesn't look too unhappy about it.

'Because it's cold as a penguin's toe, and despite your chilling appearance, you are officially the second-warmest member of Club Loser. I've tested everyone.'

'Second warmest?' Colette raises an eyebrow. 'And also, tested how?'

'Yes, Halster's the warmest because of the burning rage inside her. But she just sat on the puke seat, so I'm not snuggling up to her,' Gus says.

I give Hallie a comforting pat on the shoulder as I take the seat behind her. 'Unlucky, Hal.'

'Who'd have thought there'd be a plus side to sitting on the puke seat?' Hallie grins.

'Guys, it's been sanitised!' Mr C says again, his smile fading slightly.

'And I've spent the past year carrying out a series of highly scientific experiments to find out which of you is the best Club Loser member to be close to during any given situation,' Gus says.

'Such as?' I ask, smiling at Col as she takes

the seat next to me.

'Too cold? Hallie or Naira,' Gus says. 'Too hot? Colette or Naira again – she is a master of controlling her body temperature. Lost, stressed or need a bit of quiet? Angelo every time.'

'What about if you're sad?' Ms Huxley says.

'If it's a needing comfort kind of sad, then Col, 'cos she's the best hugger.' Gus nods like a wise mage.

'Happy with that,' Col smiles.

'If it's a brooding, brothers in arms kind of sad, then Angelo,' Gus says.

And I feel stupidly pleased.

'Why can't I be your brother in arms?' Hallie huffs. 'That's so sexist.'

'Nothing to do with gender, Hal. You just can't sit and brood like Angelo can. You get bored after, like, thirty seconds and go on your phone.'

'Any other categories?' Naira says.

Gus nods. 'I'm glad you asked, Nai-Nai. There

are many categories and sub-categories . . . for example there are thirty-two different scenarios under the zombie apocalypse heading.'

It's mad how well we've got to know each other since our fateful Saturday detention, back in the early days of Year 7 at Dread Wood High. When I arrived at school that day to see Naira, Gus and Hallie at the gates, all I wanted was to get through the detention with as little chat as possible. We had nothing in common. No reason to be friends. But being attacked by the Latchitts and their genetically mutated giant spiders forced us together, and that's when I realised they were the kind of people I'd trust with my life. No matter how different we are, we have the things that matter in common. And when Colette joined the group, it made Club Loser complete.

'Let's hear them, Gus,' I say. The way Gus's mind works is fascinating. It's like he sees the world as scenes from the craziest movies blended with real life. With added blood and sparkles.

'Shall we discuss them on the way?' Mr C says, starting the engine.

'Dare I ask where we're going for my surprise birthday trip that has started with the Dread Wood High minibus, complete with custom banner?' Colette says.

This is a question we all want to know the answer to.

'Only the most exciting hang-out in Finches Heath!' Ms Huxley says, as the tyres start rolling forward on the crunchy gravel.

'And whose definition of "best" are we using here?' Colette says. 'Because Mr C's version of best is . . .'

'The wetlands centre.' Mr C nods without taking his eyes off the road.

'Oh god, it's not the wetlands centre, is it?' Naira says. 'It's too cold to be dealing with nature, and these trainers are new.'

'Fear not,' Mr C says. 'The venue we have

chosen for this thirteenth birthday extravaganza is . . . drum roll, please . . .' Ms Huxley bangs her hands on the dash, and the rest of us brace ourselves. 'The place where all the cool kids go – the Neon Perch!'

Col's mum turns around to see our reactions.

'Hold on,' Hallie says. 'That actually *is* the place where all the cool kids go. Are you pranking us?'

'Please don't be pranking us.' Gus is jiggling in his seat. 'For the love of all that is great and good in this world – wireless headsets, grilled halloumi, unlimited Wi-Fi, brand-new sicks – please don't be pranking us.'

'Are we actually?' Colette says. 'You're taking us to Neon Perch?'

'You know, I don't think they want to go, Faye,' Mr C says, grinning at us in the mirror. 'Shall we head for the wetlands centre instead?'

'Don't you dare!' Colette says.

'It was Teddy's idea,' Ms Huxley says, looking at Mr C with heart eyes. 'The sad news is that we can't hang out with you – Mr Hume has called a meeting at school, so we'll be dropping you off and then picking you up later.'

'Well, this evening has taken a surprising turn for the better,' Hallie says.

'Meeting?' Naira asks. 'Since when?'

'Don't worry, Naira, it's not compulsory for students,' Mr C says. 'It's to discuss the ongoing renovations of the school. You know, since the incident a year ago . . .'

'When we blew up the basement to destroy some genetically mutated spiders that wanted to eat us?' I ask, trying to hold in a grin because it was an epic moment.

'Yes, exactly,' Mr C says. 'As you know there was some superficial damage that needed repairing, which turned up some other structural issues to the mansion, and Mr Hume has decided to take the opportunity to carry out some additional building work.'

'Why didn't we know about this?' Naira says. I'm not sure if she's suspicious or she has some weird school meeting FOMO.

'It was only announced today,' Ms Huxley says. 'Your mum's going, don't worry.'

'How do you know Naira's mum's going?' Colette says.

Ms Huxley holds up her mobile, which is pinging with notifications. 'We made a WhatsApp group.'

'You did what?' Colette says.

'It's great,' Mr C says. 'There's both of us, obvs, plus Naira's mum, Hallie's mum, the mother and father of Mister Gustav, and of course Angelo's parents.'

'Oh god,' I say. 'Why?'

'So we can keep in touch if anything comes up,' Ms Huxley says.

'You mean, like being stuck on a sinking ship?' Hallie asks.

'Being chased by psychos in clown masks,' Colette says.

'Cannibal octopuses . . .' I say.

'Vampire birds . . .' Naira sighs.

'Or if one of us runs out of artisan crisps?' Gus nods. 'Good thinking.'

'Not that anything else bad is going to happen,' Mr C says.

'But it also means we can meet up for drinks and nibbles.' Ms Huxley smiles.

'Please don't say "drinks and nibbles", Mum,' Colette says. 'It's awful.'

'Not as bad as "picky bits",' I put in. I'm imagining what our parents are all saying in the group chat and then wishing I hadn't. 'That is the absolute worst.'

'This whole situation is a disaster,' Hallie groans.

'Shall we focus on tonight's festivities instead?' Mr C says, taking the main road that leads out of Finches Heath to the Neon Perch and freedom.

'Yes, let's,' Col's mum says. 'Prepare to bask in the greatness of my parenting when I tell you what we have in store for you all, on this most special of days for my baby girl . . .'

'Please stop, Mum,' Colette says.

'We've booked a few different activities . . .' Ms Huxley carries on, and I'm worrying about how I'm gonna pay because I only have, like, eight pounds on me, and that won't cover much at the Neon Perch except a Coke and a game of pool.

'Which we have prepaid of course,' Mr C says, like he's been reading my mind. I'm so relieved. 'And we'll give you a food and drink kitty.'

'A what now?' Gus says.

'A kitty. For noms and spends.' Mr C grins at us through the rear-view.

'Oh Jesus,' Hallie says, burying her face in her hands. 'Kill me now.'

'But then you won't get to enjoy the kitty,' Mr C says.

'First things first.' Naira raises her voice to be heard above the groaning. 'Please explain what a kitty is. It's clearly old-person language and we don't understand.'

'You know . . . a kitty,' Ms Huxley says. 'When

you get a pot of money together that you spend jointly.'

'Or, in this case, a jazzy bumbag,' Mr C says.

'Ooh, dibs I'm wearing the bumbag,' Gus says, like any of us were going to fight him for the opportunity. Gus loves any chance to dress up.

'So we get a bumbag of money to spend at the Neon Perch?' Naira says. 'And . . . this is hard to say . . . the money is for "noms and spends"?'

'Noms and spends!' Mr C says. 'Food, drinks, games, souvenirs, whatever your heart desires. The Neon Perch is your oyster.'

'I think we have a new winner for the worst thing Mr C has ever said,' Hallie says. '*Noms* is just indescribably horrible.'

'How much money is in this kitty?' Colette asks, which is a good question, because we all eat a LOT.

'Quite a bit,' Ms Huxley says. 'So take good care of it.'

'Nice!' Gus puts his hand up to high-five Ms Huxley.

'Yeah, thanks,' I say. 'That's so generous.'

'And we've prepaid for Battle Karts . . .'

'Yesss!' we all say. The go-karts are awesome.

'. . . Galactic Golf . . .'

'Excellent,' Naira says, 'cos she knows she'll destroy all of us at mini golf.

'. . . Songbird Karaoke . . .'

Gus does a little scream of happiness, and Colette's face lights up.

'. . . and – drum roll, please,' Ms Huxley says, and we all hammer our hands on the seats in front. 'The brand-new, immersive, zombie escape room experience: Project Z.'

'I think I'm gonna cry,' Gus says. 'This is like all my dreams come true.'

'Mum and Mr C, I take back every bad thing I've ever thought about you.' Colette is beaming now. 'You're the best. This is perfect.'

'Yeah, thanks so much,' I say, like a person who hardly knows any words, because I don't know what else to say. My parents could never afford this. On the rare occasion that we visit the Perch, me and Raph get to choose one activity each and we bring snacks from home. Don't get me wrong, I'm massively grateful to my parents for it – they work extra shifts and miss out on stuff for themselves so they can take us. Our family trips to the Perch are my favourite days. But being able to spend a whole evening there with my friends and not having to worry about paying for it is a real gift.

'Mr C, and – might I be so bold as to address you as the future Mrs C . . .?' Gus says. Ms Huxley goes red in the cheeks.

'You may NOT,' Colette says. 'Way too soon.'

'And why should Colette's mum change her name anyway?' Hallie says.

'Shush, you're ruining a beautiful moment,' Gus says. 'What I'm trying to say, is that you two are freaking awesome and I thank you from the bottom of my stoma bag.'

I start laughing. 'Cos it's funny, and 'cos I

have the best feeling of excitement fizzing inside me. After all the fear and dread we've experienced in the last year, it's like dancing in the water sprinklers on the school field on a boiling-hot day.

Colette squeezes my arm and smiles at me. 'Tonight is going to be perfect.'

And I totally believe it.

CHAPTER TWO

THE NEON PERCH

The skies darken as we reach the edges of Finches Heath. Mr C chugs the school minibus past the last residential areas – new-build estates giving way to a few patchy fields – and then on towards the industrial estate that sits at the bottom of Finches Hill. It rises up in a slow slope, curving towards the summit where the Neon Perch is . . . perched. It sits there, lit up like fireworks in the winter sky, hanging off the side of the hill, facing back towards town.

'There she is.' Gus sighs. 'A beacon of joy and glory.'

We all scooch closer to the windows to get a better view, safe in the knowledge that it's now too dark for anyone to see the 'peng' birthday banner below our faces. The industrial estate is a hive of activity, flashing with the lights of forklifts and the deep bellow of truck horns as they convoy in and out with their loads. Beyond them, the business park gleams under street lights; hundreds of illuminated windows framing people typing on laptops and talking at their monitors with headphones on. I imagine a life working in an office like that, all ties, swivel chairs and online meetings. I can't think of anything worse. And then there's a stretch of wild forest, a little like the Dread Wood but more pine-based, and with electricity pylons rising out of clearings in the trees. It's like a band of human-less dark green forming a buffer between the work-busy area at the base of the hill, and the fun-busy Perch at the top.

The Neon Perch is everything you'd imagine it to be: a vision of pink and yellow electrical vibrancy, lighthousing out of its dreary surroundings. It's an enormous, colosseum-shaped building, but with one section at the top cut away and wrapped in glass, so that it's open to the sky and gives the best view of Finches Heath possible, considering it's just a boring town made up of mostly ugly buildings.

'She doesn't have the retro charm of the fairground, but she's a close second,' Gus says.

'The Perch is way better than the fair,' Naira says. 'You can go on the equipment without fearing for your life because they actually safety test it.'

'Don't be hating on the fair, Nai-Nai,' Gus says. 'You're just salty 'cos the Latchitts made it into a hellscape last time we went.'

'Well, yeah.' Naira rolls her eyes.

'There are better food options at the Perch,'

Hallie says. 'And the toilets are nicer.'

'Important points, Halster, but my heart will always rule my head in these situations. For right or for wrong.' Gus lets out a long sigh, like his heart has led him into many life-defining moments.

'Let's just hope our night at the Perch doesn't turn out like our night at the fair,' Colette says.

'Impossible,' Mr C says, taking the bends in the road that leads up the hill way more slowly than necessary. 'The Latchitts are locked up, sussy Hume will be at school with us . . .'

'Don't say "sussy",' Hallie cuts in. 'It's not appropriate for a man of your age.'

'And you are free to celebrate your first triumphant steps into teenagehood,' Mr C carries on.

'If we ever make it up this hill,' I say. There's a queue of traffic behind us and I can see a couple of rude hand gestures aimed in our direction.

I'm impatient to get there too. To step into the Neon Perch and have fun with my friends. To eat too much food, to crash go-karts, to laugh until we hurt. And finally, five minutes later, although it feels like much longer, Mr C pulls the minibus into the car park.

'Have the best time.' Ms Huxley waves at us as we pile out of the van. 'We'll be back here at nine unless you need us sooner.'

'No chance.' Colette grins, taking the bumbag of spending money from her mum and passing it straight to Gus.

'Kitty is a beauty.' Gus strokes it, and straps it across his shoulder like a roadman.

'Thanks so much, Mum, Mr C.' Colette waves. 'Love you.'

We all snigger of course and Colette swears. 'That last part was meant for Mum. Sorry, Mr C, but we're not there yet.'

'Don't worry, I love you, Mr C,' I laugh, and I blow him a kiss that he mimes catching and putting in his pocket.

'We all do!' Gus whoops. 'Guardians of Colette, we thank you for bestowing upon us a night of unsupervised fun at the Neon Perch.'

'Yeah, thank you.' Naira smiles, and I swear even she looks excited.

'You did good for old people.' Hallie grins. 'Thanks.'

And as the automatic doors slide open and welcome us in to be greeted by the beeps and flashes of the arcade machines, that feeling of delicious freedom grows with each step.

We pause on the threshold, taking it all in. The unpixellated beauty of the gaming station. The smell of tacos and pizza. The polished path ahead that will lead us to the bowling alley, the go-karts, the ice rink, the VR and karaoke rooms. So many options. There are quite a few people around, but it's nowhere near as packed as it gets on the weekend.

'Where first?' Naira says. 'Your birthday, your choice, Colette.'

'Battle Karts, before they get busy. Then we

can really smash each other up.' Colette's already jogging ahead.

'That's my girl,' I grin and jog after her. The others follow, and we make our way to the left of the ground floor, which is mostly taken up by the go-kart track, bordered on one side by the bowling alley and on the other by the American diner that is producing some amazing melted cheese and grilled meat smells.

'We have to take a selfie before we all get helmet hair,' Hallie says, and she makes us pose by the Battle Karts sign for a bunch of goofy shots.

And then we Battle Kart, which is about as close to Mario Kart in real life as you're gonna get. For twenty minutes we have the track to ourselves, and we whizz around, being overly competitive, whooping and colliding, until we've had the wind knocked out of us about a hundred times. Hallie terrorises everyone, of course. Her 'no fear' strategy is high risk, high reward, and I know I'm going to have neck ache tomorrow from her go-karting at me like a raging bull.

'I wish I could drive one of these around in real life,' she says when our time is up and we're stood at the side of the track, taking off our helmets and trying to get our breath back.

'The rest of us would be roadkill,' Gus says. 'They'd be peeling corpses off the tarmac everywhere you went.'

Hallie grins like she's not against the idea, and thumps her helmet across the counter to the bored-looking guy behind it. 'What's next?'

We get drinks and waste some money in the arcade while we finish them. Then we bowl (Naira wins the first match, Col wins the second and I pull off an astounding victory in round three). When we emerge from the lanes, it's almost six and we're starving, so we head to Uccellino's for the best pizza in Finches Heath, cramming it in our mouths while the Neon Perch starts to fill up around us.

'What's next on the list?' Hallie asks through a mouthful of pizza.

'Please say Project Z,' Gus says, doing the praying-hands thing.

Colette nods. 'Mum told me that Project Z is booked for six thirty so we need to hurry.'

'Yessss!' we all say, because Project Z is definitely the star of the Neon Perch's show. It's new, so none of us have done it before.

I make sure every plate is clear before we leave the restaurant, because I was brought up to believe that wasting food is a punishable crime, then we pay the bill and hurry back over to the escalators that will take us down to the basement. We're on such a high. Buzzing from the fun and the food, and impatient to get to Project Z.

'Do you think there will be real zombies?' Gus asks. 'I hope there's real zombies. Like, we've had to fight loads of terrifying creatures but never zombies. How is that fair?'

'Remind me who you want to be next to if

you're trapped in an escape room with a zombie,' I say.

'Hallie for sure.' Gus nods. 'She'll go straight in for an attack, and I can get the hell out of there while they're eating her.'

'I feel like Project Z is going to bring out the worst in some of us,' Naira says, side-eyeing Gus.

'Nah, it's going to be the best thing ever.' Colette's face is so pink and happy, and I love to see it. 'Because it's my birthday and nothing can go wrong.'

And I want to yell that no one should ever say that, because in the movies – and also many of our recent experiences – it always means that something is about to go massively, horribly, terrifyingly wrong. But I remind myself that Col's right. The Latchitt horror is over. We're in the clear. Nothing can go wrong . . . can it?

CHAPTER THREE

PROJECT Z

The basement in the Perch has a totally different look to the upper floors. It's dimly lit and constructed with dull metallic walls giving off bunker vibes. There are chunky pipes and electrical cables running along the walls and across the ceiling, and dark and dingy doorways that are the perfect place for monsters to lurk. It's so quiet after the blaring music that we have just left, which should be kind of nice, 'cos I'm not a fan of loud places, but it's actually really creepy. There's the sound of water dripping, though I can't see any, and every now and then the bang of metal on metal, which makes us all jump. Some parts of it are barricaded with corrugated steel and 'Danger: Do Not Enter' tape, and I'm not sure if it's to add to the atmosphere or because there's still building work going on. Whatever – it makes the nervous tension inside me start to build.

We follow the signs to Project Z, winding through a maze of corridors that all look exactly the same, until we reach some shiny sliding doors that look out of place among the dull surroundings.

A stern-looking lady in a lab coat and glasses looks up at us from behind a desk as we walk in.

'Welcome to Project Z. Please enter your names into the system so we can ensure you have security clearance.'

We type our names into a touchscreen mounted on the wall by the desk. It scans us one by one and takes our photos, then announces that we have passed all the checks and may enter the facility. The woman watches us coldly while this is happening, and I know it's immersive and part of the game, but I feel myself getting more and more uncomfortable.

'When you step through the door into the facility, security is paramount. You leave your real identities here and become anonymous . . .'

'Ooh, exciting,' Gus says. 'Can I give myself a code name? I'm gonna choose Rick Steel, and my personality will be –'

'You have been assigned code names and you must use them for the duration of your tour,' she interrupts, holding a freshly printed stack of security passes with our photos on. 'From this point on you will be known as . . . Victor.' She hands Hallie her badge. 'November.' That's Naira. 'Echo.' Colette takes her pass. 'Romeo.' She hands mine to me and I can't help feeling a bit smug.

Hallie and Naira roll their eyes.

'You lucked out there,' Gus says. 'What's

mine? What's mine? What's mine?'

'You are Golf.' The lady gives him his pass.

'Not gonna lie, I'm a bit disappointed,' Gus says, clipping the badge to his hoodie. 'But I'll make it work.'

'This way,' the lady says, and she directs us through a restricted access door into a waiting area. The door closes quietly behind us.

We automatically stand in a defensive huddle – because there's nowhere to sit, and because there are dark green metal doors on every wall around us that seem strangely hostile.

'Anyone else feel like we're about to be marched into Mr Hume's office to get a lecture?' Hallie says. 'Like, this is super tense.'

'It really is.' Colette giggles nervously.

'Better warm up,' Gus says, doing some ridiculous lunges and making the rest of us snigger. 'What?' he says. 'You'll regret not joining me when you pull a muscle and get eaten by the undead.'

'I wish they'd just let us get started,' Naira

says. 'The waiting around is making me nervous. Bring on the physical, mental and psychological challenges, you cowards!' She shakes a fist at the security camera watching us from the corner of the room, and we all laugh, 'cos Naira doesn't do the funny stuff often, but when she does it's like an unexpected gift.

And then an alarm starts screeching all around us, making us flinch and squeal and immediately stop laughing. A jet of smoke blasts down from a vent in the ceiling, filling the room with weird-smelling fog. One of the doors flies open and a guy and a woman, both of them absolute units and wearing army fatigues with massive guns strapped across their chests, burst into the room with a shout.

'This is a code red,' the guy, whose name badge says *Yonko*, yells at us.

'There's been a breach,' the woman – *Slayer* – roars, looking at us like we've just kicked her pet duck. 'The facility has been compromised.'

'Should we leave?' Gus says, edging towards the door we entered through.

'It's too late for that,' Yonko says. 'The only way out is through the facility. And you'll have to be tested.'

'For what exactly?' Hallie puts her hands on her hips.

'To make sure you haven't been infected,' Slayer snaps back. They glare at each other, and I feel like this could be the ultimate battle between two Titans.

'Our job is to get you to the testing zone alive,' Yonko shouts. 'If you make it, you'll have to face a series of physical, psychological and mental challenges, all designed to distinguish the living . . .' he pauses a moment for dramatic effect, 'from the dead.'

'Now *that's* what I'm talking about,' Gus whoops.

'If you pass the tests you might just make it out of the facility,' Slayer shouts. 'But from the look of you whelps, I sure doubt it.'

'Who are you calling a whelp?' Hallie says.

'And why have you just turned Texan?' Colette asks, trying not to laugh. 'I swear your accent was, like, Cockney, when you first came in.'

'We don't want to hear no talking!' Yonko screams in Colette's face.

'And we don't want to hear no cursin', no screamin' or no cryin',' Slayer barks at Hallie who looks like she's taking it as a personal challenge.

'Now if you want to survive, get your good-for-nothing butts down this corridor without looking back.' Yonko opens one of the doors and points us into the darkness ahead.

'Erm, after you.' I gesture for him to go first, less because it's polite and more because I don't want to run into a pitch-black zombie lab.

'Move yourself, Romeo!' Yonko roars, and I figure I'm going to have to do it or he'll just keep shouting at me, and I don't want any more spit spray in my face.

'Yeah, all right, man, calm yourself down,' I say.

'Why is he so angry?' Colette's trying so hard not to giggle, I can tell.

'Did we tell you to speak, Echo?' Slayer shouts in her face, and that just makes it worse. Col is shaking with held-in laughter.

'Now get your civilian butts down that corridor.' Slayer pulls the assault rifle off her shoulder and makes a show of ejecting the ammo magazine and clicking a new one into place. 'We'll cover you.'

'Go! Go! Go!' Yonko yells, and I jog into the dark passageway, knowing there will be a zombie waiting for me up ahead.

It's hard to run when you don't know where you're going and you can't see anything, but I figure that nothing bad is actually going to happen, so I plunge forward, hearing Col giggling behind me, and the thunk of feet on metal as everyone else follows.

'Get down!' Slayer yells suddenly, and strobe

lights flash to illuminate a zombie in a lab coat lurching at me from a doorway on my right. It screeches and snarls and claws at me with bloody hands. I can't see too well because of the mental lighting, but it looks authentic enough to give me a proper scare. I dodge to get out of its reach, stumbling into Col, and we both fall into the opposite wall as the sound of rifle fire explodes around us. There are more jets of that disgusting-smelling gas, and the zombie falls backwards into the dark.

'We got Zs coming at us from all directions,' Yonko says. 'You need to move. Now!'

And we're up and running again.

'Take a left,' Slayer yells, and I fling myself left, turning back as gunshots ring out again and Yonko and Slayer shoot at a horde of zombies coming from behind.

'Yonko!' Slayer screams. 'God damn it, Yonko, stay with me!'

But Yonko screams and is dragged off by zombies.

'This is awesome,' Gus says.

Colette is still laughing.

'Let me have a crack at them,' Hallie says to Slayer, who's running to catch up with us. 'You got a spare weapon?'

'Civilians aren't authorised.' Slayer glares at her.

'That really doesn't make any sense in a life-or-death situation,' Naira says. 'Could it be because your weapons are just plastic toys?'

'Shush, Naira, you'll ruin the magic,' Gus says.

'Just move,' Slayer says. 'Right at the end of the corridor, to the lift. Hit the button to go down. I'll keep 'em off our backs.'

So we run some more, until we find the lift where a large button with a down arrow on it is lit up like a 3 a.m. notification on your phone.

'If the electricity is working, you'd think they'd just turn the lights on,' Naira says, as I punch the button.

'I think you're supposed to ignore the obvious

plot holes in a place like this, Nai.' I smile. 'Or the whole thing would just seem ridiculous.'

'I know, I know,' Naira says. 'But I mean, come on. That's just sloppy work.'

'Naira,' Gus says. 'Do you remember when we talked about the good version of clichés: gleeches?'

'Overdone classics?' Colette says. 'Like, it having to be dark in a zombie-infested building?'

'Like, literally every sentence that came out of Slayer and Yonko's mouths?' Hallie sighs. The lift is taking ages and there's no sign of Slayer.

'Exactly,' Gus says. 'The reason they're overdone is because they're so good. We want them. We welcome them. They are gleeches.'

'This whole place is going to be full of them,' I say. 'So you might as well embrace it.'

Slayer runs around the corner towards us, just as the lift pings and the doors slide open. 'Get in!' she screams. 'They're right on my tail.'

So we bundle into the lift, Slayer behind us, and turn to face the doors as they're sliding shut. As they inch closed, the strobe lights kick off again, and two zombies appear a few metres away.

'Come on.' Slayer smashes at the lift door button. 'Come on!'

'Gleeche.' Gus smiles, as the zombies get closer.

'COME ON!' Slayer yells. The zombies are almost in touching distance, just as the doors close.

'Thank god.' Slayer turns towards us, 'Now here's what you need to do next . . .'

Without warning, the doors shoot open and two sets of zombie hands grab Slayer from behind. One of the zombies is huge, the other one small and wiry. Slayer's eyes go wide as the zombies grasp her around the torso and yank her backwards. Her feet scrabble at the floor, desperately trying to get some purchase, but she's slipping. I have half a second to think about trying to help – maybe taking her gun and firing at the zombies. But the small zombie knocks the weapon out of her hand and it clatters into the corridor – I can't see where exactly because of the smoke and lights. Then Slayer is dragged out of the lift by the two zombies, thrashing and screaming.

'There's not much time . . . save yourselves!' she gasps. Although, to be fair, and I feel a bit bad about it, none of us were making much of an attempt to risk our lives to help her.

As the lift doors start to close again, and the fake horror scene in front of us grows smaller with each centimetre, the two zombies raise their faces and look straight at us. It's only for a second, and the lights and smoke make everything confusing. But for a heartbeat I could swear they look like the Latchitts.

CHAPTER FOUR

IN THE DARK

The doors close, and they're gone, and I instantly start doubting myself. I know the Latchitts are locked up so they can't be here. I guess the trauma of everything they put us through runs deep, and I'll probably always think I see them in random places.

'That was intense,' Hallie says. 'Almost seemed real.'

There's a dim light on in the lift, so we can see each other's shocked faces.

'I know Yonko and Slayer were jerks,' Gus

41

nods. 'But you have to admire their commitment to their roles.'

'And the zombies were actually quite scary,' Colette says with a shiver. She's stopped giggling and I wonder if she's thinking what I was thinking. The others look pale too. Maybe we're all hallucinating zombie Latchitts. I don't want Col's birthday to be ruined by bad memories, so I decide to bury my fears and try to bring the fun back.

'Wasn't it a terrible coincidence that Slayer got taken just as she was about to give us some very important instructions?' I snigger.

'Almost like they planned it that way,' Naira agrees.

'Gleeche, Naira. Gleeche.' Gus pats her on the back. 'Learn to love them.'

'Really, you should be calling me by my code name,' Naira says. 'So it's November to you . . .' she bites back a laugh, 'Golf.'

'Why did I get the suckiest name?' Gus says. 'It's so unfair. And whose idea was it to use

Golf as a code name? It's lame.'

'It's the NATO alphabet, Golf.' Naira rolls her eyes. 'Each letter has a word connected to it so nobody gets confused.'

'Oh, like when people use walkie-talkies.' Gus's face lights up again. 'That's actually quite cool.'

The lift keeps trundling downwards. I don't know if it's actually moving or just made to feel like it is, but the sensation of being lowered deeper and deeper underground is chillingly realistic.

'So they gave me Golf 'cos I'm Gus, and you November 'cos you're Naira,' Gus says.

'I'm not sure that's it,' Naira says. 'Because the others don't follow. Angelo would be Alpha . . .'

'Another fitting codename for me,' I grin.

'What's C?' Colette says.

'Chupacabra,' Gus says. 'It's got to be.'

'It's not Chupacabra,' Naira says. 'It's Charlie.'

'How far are we going in this lift?' Hallie says.

'Clearly all the way to the depths of hell,' Colette says. 'Where the chupacabras roam.' She grins at Gus. And I'm thinking how good it is to see her smile like that, when a blast of weird-smelling fog hisses into the lift from a device on the ceiling. Then the lights flicker and go out, leaving us in pitch-black darkness.

'Guys?' Hallie says, and someone grabs my arm. I instinctively reach for Colette, my hand feeling for hers while I try not to think about being trapped in such a small space.

'This you, Romeo?' Gus says, pinching my arm.

'Yeah, thanks for that.' I'm still fumbling for Col's hand.

'And that must make this bony arm November's,' Gus says. 'I can tell from the dagger elbows.'

'You'll get a dagger elbow in your ribs if you don't stop pinching me,' Naira says.

'I've got you, I think, Col,' Hallie says. And I let out a sigh of relief as my hand finally makes contact with a familiar one. I squeeze it tight, and it squeezes back.

'Everyone OK?' Colette says.

'Peachy,' Hallie says. And I can hear the eye-roll.

'Something just touched my foot,' Naira says. 'Was it one of you?'

'Not me,' Gus says.

'Or me,' Hallie says. 'You think this is part of the game?'

I feel a sudden weight on my foot, there and gone in a second. Like something ran over the top of it. Not human. And my mind is racing, because surely they don't use animals as part of Project Z? It's a strictly zombie versus human situation. Unless there are zombie animals in here too – escaped lab bunnies or something.

'You hear that?' Naira says – always the sharpest ears.

We fall quiet and listen.

And I hear it. The scritch scratch of nails or claws against the corrugated metal walls of the lift. And there's the lingering smell of the gas that blasted us just before it went dark. It's different from the zombie smoke – kind of fresh, like a cool breeze has drifted in from the outside. Except we're in a two-metre square, sealed steel box. There shouldn't be anything coming in from outside. Then I feel something against my right leg. An unpleasant warmth like there's something down there, breathing on me.

'Nai's right,' I say. 'We're not alone.'

'Tell me where it is, and I'll kick it,' Hallie says. And there's a moment of confused shuffling as we try to huddle up, but it's so totally dark that we just end up bumping into each other. For a split second the lift light flashes on – a sudden, unnatural yellow glow that illuminates everything around us in a weird way, the colours strange and everything muffled by a heavy mist. It's almost like I'm watching the scene in a dream. And in that moment, though I don't have time to focus, I catch a glimpse of us all reflected in the metal wall. It's not a perfect mirror, so the shapes are distorted – stretched in some places, squeezed in others. And the light goes out again before I can properly take it all in, leaving me shaking. Because I saw something so wrong that it's like the contents of my chest have sunk like stones into the pit of my stomach. I didn't see five people reflected in the lift wall. I saw six.

CHAPTER FIVE

ON THE CLOCK

I try to reform the picture in my mind and make it make sense, zooming in on each figure in the reflection to work out which one didn't belong. Naira on the far right – still the tallest, her sleek black ponytail swinging as she turns to look around her. Then Gus – once the smallest of us but filling out and getting noticeably taller by the day. His light hair bright yellow in the electric light. Then there's me, Colette, Hallie. And – though I know it's impossible – Colette again. She's on both sides of Hal. But how can she be on both sides of Hal?

And she drops my hand.

'Col,' I say. 'You OK?'

The lift fills with the sound of scratching and scuttling – the metal box amplifying every tiny noise so that it feels like it's all around us.

'Erm, as OK as I can be in this horrific situation,' she says.

'Why'd you let go of my hand?' I say, and I feel sick waiting for her answer 'cos I'm already half expecting what it's going to be.

The light flickers again, and this time it stays on, casting its glow over the five of us in the lift. Naira, Gus, me, Hallie and Colette, all looking down at the floor, trying to catch a glimpse of whatever was running around a few moments ago. And yeah, the creature noises are worrying me, but the thing that's bothering me most is the figure I saw reflected on the wall.

'I wasn't holding your hand,' she says. 'Only Hallie's.'

'There was someone else here,' I say, feeling suddenly way too hot and like there isn't enough air.

Gus puts his hand on my shoulder. 'There was definitely something in here with us, but it was giving me more creepy animal vibes. Like mega zombie kittens or something.'

'Yes, there was a creature,' I say, and I'm looking around the walls of the lift to try to work out where it could have got in and out. 'But I'm telling you there was a person too. I thought it was Colette, but it wasn't.'

Then the lift pings and the doors start to open, and I'm already doubting what I saw. But I turn my focus to the sliding doors for a moment, 'cos who knows what's waiting for us there.

Hallie steps forward and rolls back her shoulders. 'I'll go first. We might need to fight our way out.'

But the area outside the lift is quiet and empty. No alarms, no flashing lights or jets of smoke, no zombies. And that somehow feels worse than stepping into a war zone. The silence is creepy as hell. All I can see is a green door with a digital clock above it.

'Oh god,' Naira says, darting towards the door. 'We're on a countdown. And we have just under forty-five minutes to get out of here.' She points at the clock.

'That would make sense,' I say. 'Seeing as this is an escape room and Slayer said we don't have much time. But I just need to check the lift – try to work out how whatever or whoever was in there with us got in.'

But the lift doors have closed, and apparently me banging on the button won't make them open again.

'It's probably part of the experience,' Naira says. 'And we really need to hurry, because the timer is counting down and it's making me uncomfortable.'

'So if we don't finish this in time we'll be fake locked in?' Hallie rolls her eyes. 'Big deal.'

'But it would mean we failed,' Naira says, powering through the door like she's late for an exam. 'And that's just unacceptable.'

'You know, I've watched millions of videos on the internet where they do these lift pranks,' Gus says, putting his hand on my shoulder. 'There's like a secret panel in the side where someone hides. The lights turn off, they sneak out and jump-scare everyone. It was probably that.'

'Yeah, maybe,' I say. I've seen those videos too. 'But if it was all part of the experience, why not put a zombie in there? It doesn't make sense.'

Gus follows the others through the door and I follow.

'Maybe there's some kind of alternative story at work and it will all become clear as we play on,' Gus says.

I try to put it to the back of my mind so I can

focus on the game.

We're in an old-fashioned office with wood-panelled walls and a leather-topped desk and chair in one corner. An ancient computer and monitor are sat, gathering dust on the desk, surrounded by files of papers and posh pens. Around the edges of the room there are shelves of books and sculptures and oil paintings of a sailing ship, a historical marketplace with strangely hatted gentlemen selling corn and cows, and what looks like a 1920s county fair. The floor is covered in a huge red and gold patterned rug and fake potted plants stand in the corners. On the opposite side of the room is another door.

I hold the door we came in through open, reluctant to let it shut in case it locks us in. It feels wrong to knowingly put ourselves in a trap.

Naira has already run to the opposite door and is reading a notice on it. '*The exit can only open when the entrance is closed*. You've got to shut the door, Angelo. It's a one-way system.'

'But I feel like I don't want to?' I say.

'We can't go back anyway,' Hallie says. 'The lift wouldn't work, remember?'

'They said the only way out is through.' Colette puts her hand on my shoulder. 'I think we have to follow the rules.'

I hesitate, my hand still keeping the door open.

'You know they're going to keep banging on at you till you give in, Romeo,' Gus says, making his way around the back of the desk to sit in the spinny chair. 'At this point we're just wasting time.'

And he's right, I know.

'For god's sake, just shut it!' Naira half yells, half screams, clearly feeling the time pressure. And I let it go, trying to ignore the ominous click it makes as it closes.

'Ooh, the computer screen just switched on,' Gus says. 'This is it, Club Loser, let the games commence.'

We gather around the computer screen as it whirrs slowly into life. The image reveals pixel by pixel – so painful to watch.

'How did people live this way?' Naira sighs.

'I think it's a crossword for us to fill out,' Gus says. He's leaning back in the chair with his feet up on the desk. 'Classic escape room stuff.'

'I'm good at crosswords.' Naira manages a small smile. 'But where are the clues?'

'Must be hidden around the room.' Colette pulls at one of the desk drawers. 'Let's get searching.'

'Not yet,' Naira says. 'First rule of exams: always read the question properly. Twice. We need to wait for instructions.'

'But . . .' Colette says.

'We wait,' Naira snarls.

So we wait.

Under the crossword grid, a message appears – one letter at a time, of course:

RANSACK: To unlock the exit, find the clues and complete the crossword.

To be fair to Colette, she manages not to say anything as she opens the drawer she was going to open a whole wasted minute ago and starts rummaging inside.

'I'll check the books,' Gus says. 'There's always a hollowed-out book. Gleeche!'

The rest of us start in different areas of the room, checking in, on and under everything we can think of.

'Got one!' Colette says. 'It says *London epidemic . . .*'

'Covid!' Gus shouts and rushes to the computer to type it in.

'Don't you dare touch that keyboard,' Naira yells. 'What did I just say?'

Gus looks up, his finger hovering over a key. 'Always read the question properly?'

'Exactly,' Naira sighs.

We all look at Colette.

'*. . . of the seventeenth century.*'

'So not Covid?' Gus says.

'The Plague.' Naira sighs. 'See if it fits.'

'Plague fits.' Gus nods. 'On with the search!' And he finds a clue in the next book he opens. 'Told you!' He waves the piece of paper around.

'Read it,' Naira says. 'We don't have much time.'

'I think I know it,' Gus says. 'It says *The building blocks of all living things*.'

'Cells,' the rest of say at the same time.

'Yeah, that's what I was going to say.' Gus stuffs the clue in his pocket and his cheeks go pink. 'Totally.'

We find clues behind one of the paintings, inside a model of the human brain, and stuck at the back of one of the desk drawers. They give us 'bite', 'poison' and 'death'.

'Cheery old crossword, this,' Gus says, as he starts rolling back the rug on the floor.

'Helpful that there's a theme.' Colette is emptying the contents of the bin on to the floor.

'This one's "DNA",' Naira says, waving a strip of paper that she just dug out of the soil in one of the potted plants.

'Aren't you going to share the clue?' Gus says, looking up from his rug-rolling.

'No time,' Naira huffs. 'Don't question me. Someone just type it in.'

'You're scarier than the Halk when you're like this, you know,' Gus says.

'Yeah, you're scarier than me,' Hallie says.

I don't know where else to look, so I help Colette go through the trash, which isn't an activity I thought we'd ever be doing together. I'm thinking about the answers to clues we've solved and I have that unsettling feeling again. I mean, yeah, they're all relevant to the zombie situation, but they're also relevant to the whole Latchitt disaster we've been through. I think back to the two zombies outside the lift, trying to filter out all the distractions in the scene and picture them clearly. The shape and size of them fitted the Latchitts. The way they looked up at us was horribly familiar. But beyond that I can't be sure. Even now though, as I'm looking for clues,

I could swear I see movement through the cracks in the floorboards. I lean down for a closer look, and then my eyes fall on a tiny ball of paper wedged in one of the gaps.

'Here's something,' I say, unfolding the paper. It looks the same as the other clues. 'But it just says *RUN* in caps.'

'There's a three-letter space left.' Hallie looks at the screen. 'Run would fit. Should I type it?'

There's a sudden bang against the entrance door, followed by some scraping and screeching. The door shakes in its frame.

'Type it,' I say, getting off the floor and pulling Colette up after me.

There's another loud bang, and whatever's outside trying to get in, manages to break the wood, sending splinters flying. Then the barrage of blows stops for a moment and I turn to see why. There's a narrow split in the door, and I have this shuddery feeling that someone – *something* – is standing just the other side of it, watching and listening. I move closer.

'What are you doing, Angelo?' Naira says. 'We need to go forward, not backwards. You're going to slow us down.'

'Just want to check something,' I say. Because it seems strange to me that a zombie desperate to eat us would stop for a little think halfway through breaking down the door.

'Well, hurry,' Naira says. 'And Hallie, just type it.'

'Typing it!' Hallie yells.

The split in the wood of the door is too narrow to see anything through, so I put my ear to it instead, trying to make out if anyone's lurking behind it. For a second there's nothing, and then I hear it: soft but heavy breathing. Wafts of moist warmth seep through the crack on to my cheek, and I pull my face away in disgust. There's someone out there for sure, so why aren't they attacking?

Then a green light flashes over the room, and the exit door slides open.

'Go!' Naira yells, and I know we need to move on, or she's going to freak out. So I run with the others, out of the exit door, which swooshes shut behind us. We turn to face the next room.

CHAPTER SIX

BEND OR BREAK

We're in a dimly lit corridor with an exit door about ten metres ahead of us. To our left is another door, and next to that is a chunky monitor about the size of an iPad but five decades older, displaying a message:

BEND OR BREAK: Only one may enter. This game requires agility and balance. Choose your player wisely.

'I don't like the idea of us splitting up,' I say.

'But we have to, so we can get out . . .' Hallie says.

'Can they stop us if two of us go in, though?' I say. 'We should at least stay in pairs.'

'We have just under thirty-six minutes left – there's no time to argue,' Naira says, pushing on the door. 'I'm doing it and you're staying here.' And she's in before I can say anything else.

'Naira is peak Naira today,' I say, staring at the closed door between us.

'Look, we can watch her on the screen,' Colette says, and the rest of us stand around it, looking at a grainy feed of Naira in the corner of a small room, walking to the back wall, where she stops and looks at something we can't see. Then she jumps and lets out a scream.

'It says you guys can hear me,' Naira shouts. 'It's a laser maze. I have to get through without touching any of them in order for us to proceed to the next challenge.

'So get through laser maze, exit room. Sounds easy,' Gus says. 'Ooh, there's a button here.' He already has his finger on it. 'Maybe if we press it, we can talk back.' He presses it. 'November, November, do you read? Over.'

'I hear you,' Naira says.

'Why'd you scream just now?' Colette asks.

'There was a jet of smoke again, like in the lift,' Naira says. 'It smells minty.'

'Weird choice for a zombie experience,' Gus says, still with his finger on the intercom button. 'Why do we think . . .?'

'Shut up, Gus, I need to concentrate,' Naira yells.

'I don't think she wants us to contribute,' I snort.

In the corner of her room, Naira takes the band out of her ponytail and starts coiling her hair up.

Colette gasps. 'She's going for a bun. That's winning thinking right there.'

'Supreme. Hair. Evolution,' Gus says. 'What a hero.'

'Let's get this over with,' Naira says. Then she ducks low and carefully raises a leg, lifting it over a laser beam that we can't see. She shifts her body weight, then pulls her other leg up and over. 'That's one,' she says.

'Good skills, Nai,' Gus says with his finger on the intercom button.

Naira flinches. 'Can someone please keep Gustav away from whatever he's using to communicate with me?'

Gus retracts his finger and puts his hand in his pocket. 'Doesn't need words of encouragement. Roger that.'

We watch Naira as she progresses across the room, gracefully twisting and turning and holding poses that look like they'd make a weaker person give in to the thigh burn.

'She's magnificent,' Gus sighs.

'Defo the best person for the job,' Hallie agrees.

Naira is about halfway through the maze and balancing perfectly on one leg when her head suddenly twists to the left, making her wobble. She puts a hand out to stop herself from falling and must hit one of the lasers because the lights in the corridor turn red and a loud honking noise blasts out of a hidden speaker somewhere.

Naira swears. And Naira hardly ever swears.

A skull appears in the corner of our prehistoric spectating screen, and the words **STRIKE ONE. TWO LIVES REMAINING** flash up in horror-font letters.

'Erm, what happens if she loses all her lives?' Colette says. Then presses the button to speak to Naira who is back in the starting place while the room resets. 'Nai, what happens if you lose all your lives?'

'We get locked in and eaten by zombies,' Naira says. And it's like she's lost her focus. She's looking from side to side and rubbing her arms.

'What's up, Nai?' I press the button. 'Did something distract you?'

'I'm not sure,' she says. 'I thought I felt something brush past me. Not a zombie. Something smaller, like in the lift.' She bends down to tuck her jeans in her socks. 'Did you see anything on the screen?'

'No, nothing,' Colette says. 'But we can't see the lasers either. Just you.'

Naira pulls her socks up high and her sleeves down low. 'Just so nothing can crawl in,' she says.

'You think there's actually something there with her?' Gus says. 'This is bad.'

Hallie takes over the button. 'Nai, they probably just have some special effects to make you think there's something with you. There's no way they'd put an actual animal in the room. You can do this.'

'It felt real.' Naira retwists her bun and pulls the hairband tightly around it. 'Just like it did in the lift. But I'm going again. No way am I being beaten by a mediocre escape room prank.'

'That's our Nai,' Colette says. And we all start chanting, 'Naira, Naira, Naira . . .'

'Shut up!' Naira shouts, so we let go of the button and watch her second attempt at the maze.

She gets past the first few lasers even faster on this go. There are a couple of times where I see her flinch slightly but she keeps control and doesn't mess up. When she gets to the middle she speeds past the bit where she went wrong the first time. Then she pauses. Scratches her neck. And I think about that itch we all had when our brains were infected with the Latchitts' parasitic worms. Then my mind spirals into a panic of wondering if we're under worm control again and how it could have happened. But I stop myself because it's not helpful. I don't feel like I did back then, so I'm probably just being paranoid. It's another freak coincidence.

Naira rolls her shoulders back, then carefully

lies down on the floor so that she's as flat as she can be against the ground. Then she starts wiggling herself sideways, obviously trying to slide beneath a really low beam. We watch in silence, the tension building, and I realise that somewhere along the way we've become invested in the game. And then I hear a scratching noise – something hard and sharp clicking against the floor, or the walls.

'What's that sound?' I say, moving my face closer to the screen to see if I can spot some weird creature in the room with Naira.

'You hear it too, right?' Naira says. 'There's definitely something in here.' She bites her lip but keeps focused on moving beneath the laser beam, centimetre by centimetre. Her face is tensed into a scrunched expression that makes it look like she's in unbearable pain, and it's clear how much willpower it's taking for her to keep going. Then she turns her head like she's checking she's clear and slowly pulls herself into a crouch.

'She's shaking,' Gus whispers. 'Poor Nai.'

'Should we try to get her out?' I say, but I know the answer before the question's even out of my mouth. 'She'll hate us if we do.'

'And she's almost at the end,' Colette says.

So we watch, feeling useless, while Naira manoeuvres her way past the last few lasers, finally reaching the opposite side of the room. Then the corridor lights up green, and the maze room door opens, followed by the exit door. Naira jogs out of the room like what happened inside it wasn't some kind of psychological torture for her.

'Let's move,' she says, leading the way up the corridor to the next stage of the game.

'You want to talk about it?' Colette jogs after her.

'There was an animal in there,' Naira says. 'It was scratching and sniffing like it was deciding whether or not to eat me.'

'But it didn't hurt you?' I ask.

Naira slows. Takes a breath. 'No, it didn't.

But we need to talk about the possibility of . . .'

'. . . Latchitt sabotage,' I say.

'Surely not,' Hallie says. 'We know for a fact they're in prison.'

'They could have sent a minion to mess with us,' Gus says. We've reached the end of the corridor and are facing the next door. 'They've done it before.'

'But none of us have actually been attacked by whatever the scratchy critter is,' Hallie says. 'Plus, how would they know we'd be here? Even we didn't know we were coming until we were in the minibus.'

'Maybe we're being paranoid,' Colette says. 'We're in a busy public place, so we shouldn't be in danger. Plus the whole point of Project Z is to freak you out and challenge you. Let's just carry on for now.'

'Yeah,' Hallie says. 'Let's just get on with the next challenge so we can get out of here and play mini golf. Maybe even get another turn on the Battle Karts.'

So we run through the door, a countdown above it telling us we have twenty-seven minutes left, and I'm wondering what Project Z is going to throw at us next.

We skid into another door with a sign on it:

BUZZKILL: Game three requires strength and resilience. Two team members needed. The player from game two is not eligible. The whole team may enter and spectate. Choose your players wisely.

'This basically has my name on it,' Gus says. 'So I volunteer as tribute.'

'Me too.' Hallie nods, then pushes the door open and walks in, followed by Gus and the rest of us.

As we enter the room we're all blasted again with the mystery fog that smells of green minty medicine.

'What's with the fog showers?' Hallie says. 'Why can't we go anywhere here without getting sprayed with stinky gas?'

Of course, Gus starts giggling, but there's no time for fart jokes as we assess the scene in front of us. The room is empty except for a large metal structure running across the width of it. There are two five-foot-tall posts bolted to the floor – one on each side of the room – and running between them is a fist-thick metal wire, like a steel washing line. But the wire isn't straight, it's twisted and curved into knots and spirals and loops, like a roller coaster.

'I know what this is,' Gus says. 'I used to have one when I was little. Not one this size, obvs, but a mini one. You have to move a ring across the wire without touching it. Look, there's the ring at the base of the first post.'

'Here's the instructions,' Naira says. 'Two players must work together to move the ring from left to right. Contact with the track will have consequences – then there's a picture of a skull. The exit will open when the game is complete. All other team members must spectate only. Any interference will result in a lock-in.'

'You guys are not going to regret choosing me for this task,' Gus says. 'I'm going to annihilate it.'

'But I don't see how it requires strength and resilience.' Hallie looks at the game in disgust. 'It's just a kids' toy.'

Naira claps her hands. 'Enough talk, get started.'

'I'm excited for this. Gonna show you all my skillz.' Gus runs over to the first post and picks up the ring. It's like a big doughnut – about twenty-five centimetres in diameter and four centimetres thick. They should actually make doughnuts that size. He lifts it up the starting post and over the top so that it's circling the wire.

'Let's take it in turns and shout each other if we're getting cramps or something,' he says to Hallie.

'I won't get cramps, but whatever.' Hallie sighs. 'Tell me when you want to switch.'

'Affirmative,' Gus nods. 'I'll start.' And he moves the ring forward along the wire, quickly and confidently to the first challenging part of the course. It's a sharp ninety-degree turn to the left but at the same time slanting diagonally upwards and then into a spiral. He manages it easily, but by the time he gets to the spiral his arms are twisted up all back to front.

'Shall I take it?' Hallie says.

'No, I can do it,' Gus says. 'I just need to untangle myself.' He lets go of the ring with one hand and tries to stretch out his arm while still keeping the ring steady. But he must just clip the wire because the room lights up red, a skull is projected on to the back wall, and Gus screams like a toddler running into a patch of stinging nettles.

We all freeze, watching him as he leaps backwards away from the track, not really understanding what's happening. He's breathing fast and sweating.

Then the lights go back to normal and the

skull shrinks and moves to the corner of the wall making way for the words **Strike one. You have nine lives remaining.**

'That was dramatic,' Hallie says. 'What happened?'

'It electrocuted me,' Gus gasps. 'And not like you've been skidding across the carpet in the library and then touched something metal electrocution. It was more like those machines you get at fairgrounds where you have to see how long you can hold on while it shoots lightning bolts through you.'

'Did it hurt?' Colette makes a face.

'Hell yes,' Gus says. 'Sorry, Hal, looks like the stakes have just been raised. There's no way we're making it out of here without you and me getting fried.'

CHAPTER SEVEN

BUZZKILL

'It can't be that bad,' Hallie says. 'Let me try.' And she pulls the ring back to the start, making sure to bang it against the wire a bunch of times. 'I can't even feel anything.'

'It must switch off when you reset,' I say. 'And turn on when you start the course again.'

'Fine.' Hallie starts moving the ring along the track. She's less slick than Gus but manages to avoid contact with the wire. When she gets to the spiral, she makes sure she doesn't get twisted up like Gus did and negotiates the curves well, making it to the top without any mistakes.

'Go, Hallie,' Colette says. 'You're doing great.'

'Just wait.' Gus is standing close in case she needs help, but not close enough to get in her way.

The top of the spiral is one of the highest points of the track, and Hal has to really stretch to lift the ring over the final twist and on to the next part.

'You want me to take over? You know, as I'm taller,' Gus says with a smug look on his face.

'By like a centimetre, Gustav,' Hallie says. 'And I can do it by myself.'

'Five and a half centimetres actually,' Gus whispers.

Hallie jerks the ring forward and I hear the metallic chink as it hits the wire. The room turns red at the same time Hallie's thrown back from the track with a yell.

Strike two. You have eight lives remaining.

Hal clutches her right forearm, shouting out a bunch of swears and calling the ring track formerly known as a 'kids' toy' every offensive name she has in her back catalogue. And that's a lot.

'Told ya,' Gus says.

'How is this even legal?' Hallie says. 'Because I don't remember signing anything to say I'm OK with electric-shock therapy.'

'I don't see how it can be.' Naira pulls her phone out of her pocket like she's going to google the legal boundaries of electric shocking people, frowns, and puts it away again. 'No signal. Anyone else?'

We all check our phones, and shake our heads. Mine won't connect to anything - maybe because we're in the basement.

'Do you think Colette's mum signed something on our behalf?' Naira asks.

'I know she's a pain in my butt, but I really don't think she'd do that.' Colette's staring at the ring of doom where it's resting on the wire.

'Maybe our parents all discussed it in their WhatsApp group and decided they're OK with us being tortured,' I say. 'But like Gus said, it's not that different from the fairground strength-testing games so it must be a safe amount of electric shock, even if it feels bad. We should probably figure it out later when we're not on the clock or Naira will slap us with her ponytail.'

'Good point,' Naira says. 'Gus, Hal – are you OK to carry on?'

'We'd better teamwork this son of a gun, right?' Gus says to Hallie as he pulls the ring back to the start of the course.

'Yeah,' Hallie nods. 'Sorry I thought you were being pathetic.'

'It's all good.' Gus shrugs. 'We sigmas are often misunderstood.'

'So you should start, because you aced the first bit. I'll take it up the spiral. You lift it over and carry on, then we'll see how we go from there, yeah?' Hallie flexes her fingers and

Gus restarts the course.

They work surprisingly well as a team, with one of them holding the ring steady and the other guiding it around the crazy shapes in the wire. But two thirds of the way across is the most complicated series of twists in the track, and this time they both have their hands on the ring when it hits.

They're flung away from the course with a crack of electrical energy, Gus letting out a high-pitched scream and Hallie roaring like a lion who's just stepped on a Lego brick.

Strike three. You have seven lives remaining.

'I might be experiencing electric-shock-induced hallucinations, but was that zap stronger?' Gus says, clenching his right fist.

Hallie starts dragging the ring back to the start again. 'Yeah, I think it was worse.'

'Or maybe each shock feels more powerful because your nerves are super sensitive from the previous ones,' Naira says. And I can tell she's trying not to look at the countdown clock too obviously. Hal and Gus don't need any more pressure on them.

They try the course again and get shocked at the exact same spot. And then again.

Strike five. You have five lives remaining.

'Sorry,' Gus says. 'I keep getting these shooting pains up my arm, like they're being stabbed by a million needles, and I automatically flinch.'

'I guess this is where the resilience comes in,' Hallie growls. She's clearly taking the electric shocks personally because she looks like she wants to burn the whole place down. Both of them are pale and sweating.

'Don't worry, you can do this,' I say.

'And if you can't, it doesn't matter,' Colette adds. 'It's just a stupid game, remember. We have nothing to prove, right, Naira?' She nudges Naira who's staring at the clock again and biting her lip so hard I'm surprised it's not bleeding.

'Right.' And to be fair she puts a lot of effort into trying to smile reassuringly, even if it fails hard.

Gus snorts out a laugh. 'Nai, you look like you've just been pulled over by the police for speeding and you've got a dismembered body in the boot.'

'You actually do look exactly like that!' Colette laughs. 'Like you've got one hand resting casually on the steering wheel and the other one reaching for the shank concealed in your waistband in case he tells you to pop the trunk.'

'Finches Heath's most wanted,' Gus grins. Then he turns back to the game. 'Right. This time's the one.'

But it's not. Hallie's hand shakes when she's moving the ring over the first spiral and she screams in frustration and pain.

Nineteen minutes remaining.

'You know we can just ditch,' I say to Hallie and Gus, as they stand at the start of the wire again. 'Life is hard enough without voluntarily putting yourself through torture by electrocution.'

Gus and Hal look at each other and take hold of the ring. There's no way they're giving up, and I wonder if it's a good thing to be so damn stubborn or if it's just stupid. But I know I'd be the same. None of us would quit.

They make it past the first spiral and speed through the next few obstacles until they reach the part that looks like an infinite bundle of spaghetti.

'My nemesis,' Gus says. 'We meet again.' He takes a breath then starts moving it around the loops.

And I'm holding my breath because it's going well.

'I bet you thought you were going to destroy me,' Gus says to the wire in a growly American accent. 'You been sittin' there, all shiny and silver, with your impressive girth and powerful circuitry. You took one look at us when we mosied into this room, and you decided: you fools got no chance. You sized me up and thought: you ain't havin' this one, son. I'm gonna end you. And I'm gonna laugh when I do it . . .'

I feel Colette start shaking with silent laughter beside me.

Gus is halfway through the loops. 'Hell, I bet you've done it a thousand times. I bet for you it's as easy as walkin' through a valley with the sun on yer back and a hound at yer heels. As easy as spittin'. As easy as breathin'.' He shakes his head. Two thirds done. 'But I'm a tell you summin', you metal scumhole – you may think you know me, but you don't. You think you're gonna beat me? You think you're gonna take me down?'

He's, like, seven eighths done, and I'm laughing so hard I have tears in my eyes.

'Well, you reckoned this all wrong. 'Cos maybe you *have* been victorious a thousand times straight. Hell, maybe a million. I don't give a coyote's butt how many times you've been the last man standing. 'Cos I'm here to tell you: not today, you son of a mangy snake. Not. Today.'

And he comes cleanly out of the final loop.

'Take it,' he gasps at Hallie, and she grabs the ring and continues through the last part of the course while Gus drops into a crouch, his face in his hands.

Even Naira's laughing as Hallie makes it to the end of the wire. The room turns green and the door opens. We run into the darkness beyond, and even though I'm still laughing from Gus's monologue, I'm nervous about what's coming next.

CHAPTER EIGHT

18 MINUTES AND COUNTING

e turn a corner and reach another green door. Our instructions are displayed on an iPad mounted next to it:

POWERPLAY: The whole team must enter. One player must sit on the green stool. The other team members must each enter their named Perspex cubicle. This game will require musical skills and forgiveness.

'Musical skills and forgiveness?' Hallie frowns. 'That's a weird one.'

And none of us say it, but we all know Col is good at forgiving. Our nightmare with the Latchitts started when each one of us hurt Colette in some way and they didn't take it too well. We all regretted our actions. Apologised. Made things right. But it sticks with us, that nugget of shame. For me, no matter how much she says it's done and forgotten, it's like a bit of grit in my shoe. It pokes at me still, nudging its way into my consciousness randomly. A painful shard of a memory, cutting away at me, even on the happiest days.

'Musical skills,' Colette says, looking at the iPad. 'Like it was made for me.' She doesn't mention the other part because, like I said, she's a forgiving person.

We head into the room, and my feeling of unease, which has been growing since the incident in the lift, reaches new heights when I see what we have to do.

In the room there's a keyboard with a green stool in front of it facing four transparent plastic cubicles the size of toilet stalls. Each one has a sign with one of our code names on. I wonder how whoever set the room up knew that Colette would be the one to play the game. Maybe her mum told them she plays guitar or something.

Colette runs over to the stool, and the rest of us get into our named cubicles. The doors slide shut.

'The instructions are on the keyboard,' Colette says. Her voice is muffled by the see-through wall between us. 'I'll read them . . . *Recreate the melody you hear. If an incorrect note is played, you must start again. Errors will have consequences for your teammates.*' She looks at us in our plastic cages. 'I don't like the sound of that. What if it's more electric shocks?'

I shrug from my cubicle. 'Then we'll deal with it.'

She looks down at the instructions again and reads, '*The game will commence when the player pushes the button on the keyboard marked with a skull.*'

'Just do it,' Hallie yells from her box. 'Even though I wish Gus would stop monologuing like he's the lead in a Netflix dystopia, I have to admit he was right earlier. We can't let this game defeat us.'

'You love my monologues,' Gus yells at her. 'And I will never stop.'

She blows a kiss at him and he grins.

'Hit the skull, Colette,' Naira shouts.

Colette hits the skull and the lights in the room dim. Five spotlights flicker on, illuminating Colette at the keyboard and each of us in our cubicles. Then a tune starts playing over the speakers – a simple, familiar melody that makes my skin crawl.

'Nursery rhyme,' I gasp, and I feel a rush of panic. Wherever the Latchitts go, they take a nursery rhyme with them. Something to help control their animal creations and freak us out. It's a weird coincidence for Project Z to spin a nursery rhyme at us too. Unless the Latchitts are controlling Project Z. My eyes flick to Naira who's in the cubicle on my left, and from the look on her face I'd say she's having the same thoughts as me. This is all too much. Too familiar. Too close for comfort. I push on the door of my cubicle and find it's sealed shut.

The tune finishes playing and Colette looks down at the keyboard, trying to work out the starting note. I have no help to offer her, 'cos I don't have a clue. She bites her lip and presses one of the keys.

The lights turn red and I brace myself for an electric shock, but it doesn't come. Instead I hear a soft click and the electric whirr of something moving. I look around me, wondering what the hell is happening. There's a pressure against my back suddenly, like I'm leaning against the wall of the cubicle, but I know

I haven't moved. And if I haven't moved, it means the wall has. I try not to let the horror show on my face as I realise the sides of my cubicle are literally closing in on me. *Star Wars* trash-compactor style.

They shift by about two or three centimetres, shrinking the space around me like something straight out of my nightmares. I push the door again, and each of the walls, to stop them from moving, or to find a way out, and I feel sick with panic. Then I swear with relief as the hum of the mechanism comes to an end, and the walls stop moving.

My relief lasts less than a second as I become aware of the shrieks around me. I look to my left and see Naira huddled in the corner of her cubicle. It hasn't shrunk like mine but there are five or six big spiders scuttling across the walls. She hates spiders. I look beyond her to Gus, whose cubicle is sprayed red like someone's been murdered in there.

'Gus?' I yell, my heart dropping like a boulder

into my guts. 'GUS?'

'It's OK, it just sprayed me, like a blood shower,' Gus shouts back. 'But don't worry, I've moved Kitty to a safe place.'

I don't ask where.

'Oh my god,' Colette squeals from her stool. 'OH MY GOD!'

'What's happening in Hal's?' I yell.

'It's filling with water,' Gus shouts back. 'Her favourite.'

'She's going to drown and it'll be my fault!' Colette shouts.

'It's OK, it's stopped.' I can just make out Hallie's voice from the far cubicle.

'How come nothing happened in your cubicle?' Naira shouts.

'It did,' I say. 'It's getting smaller.'

'You mean you're getting squished?' Colette says.

'Not yet.' I smile at her, trying to be reassuring, because if she panics it's going to make her task even harder.

'You have to keep going, Colette,' Naira shouts. 'We're fine.'

Naira is clearly not fine – I can see her shaking. But she's right, Col has to keep going. And while she's doing that, I'm going to see if I can find another way out of this cubicle. Just in case.

Colette presses another key and the lights go back to safety yellow, so it must be correct. Then she sings the start of the melody . . . *'Three blind mice, three blind mice . . .'* before playing the next five notes. She gets them all correct.

I hear a repetitive thud from somewhere on my left, and I guess Hallie has decided that she needs a back-up plan too. The thing is, this plastic is tough. I start rummaging in my pockets for anything I can use as a tool.

Colette is humming the next part of the song, and some scales, and then she presses the next key. Right again. She's through *See how they run . . .* with no errors, then she hits a key and the lights turn red.

I hear Gus, Hallie and Naira scream, and below that the hum of my moving walls. I sit on the floor, my back and feet braced against opposite sides, and I push back as hard as I can. It does nothing to slow the movement, and by the time the walls stop I can only just stay in my curled-up position. The sides of my cage are uncomfortably tight around me and I feel like I can't breathe. So I get to my feet and stand straight, trying not to feel overwhelmed by the closeness of the walls.

Colette starts again and I can see tears running down her face as she plays the first part of the song perfectly and takes a second try at the note she just missed. She gets it right. But the next one – the one that jumps up high – she gets wrong.

Instead of focusing on the walls of my coffin slowly crushing me to death, I turn to look at Naira. Her cubicle is swarming with spiders and she's in a ball on the floor, her jumper pulled up over her head, doing that quiet scream that she did in Bend or Break. Gus's cubicle behind her is soaked red. I can't see Hallie's cage, but I can hear the thundering blows as she smashes it, again and again, trying to force her way out.

The plastic walls start to press either side of my shoulders, so I shift myself so that I'm standing diagonally, and then sideways, watching Naira shut down in terror. I remember that this was supposed to be a game. A fun forty-five minutes of generic challenges ending in a moment of triumph when we break free. I'm not sure exactly what's going on, but there's no doubt in my mind now that this is not a game. At least not the kind you'd choose to play.

CHAPTER NINE

NO WAY OUT

The walls stop again and I search my mind for a way out of this flaming trash fire of a situation. Colette is playing the beginning part of the tune again, and I know she's still our best shot at escaping these coffins. I focus in on the notes, but try to keep my face blank as she gets to the difficult part. I don't want her to look up and think I don't believe in her. She hesitates for a second, then hits the keys for *They all ran after the farmer's wife . . .* and this time she gets it right. I open my mouth to shout encouragement but then worry that the sound of my voice will remind her I'm about to be crushed, so I close it again and settle for sending her vibes. Which is dumb because I'm a hundred per cent certain that sending people vibes has zero impact on the outcome of their situation, no matter what Hallie says. We argue about it a lot, the vibe thing. Hal, Gus and Col are firmly on team vibe. Naira not so much. And I've always said that thinking something won't make it true. But here I am with vibes for Col and nothing else that will do any good. Maybe people like sending vibes because it's unbearable to think that there's nothing you can do to help someone.

Who cut off their tails with a carving knife . . .

I think back through everything that's happened since we entered Project Z, trying to work out the point where it all went wrong. The point where we should have realised we needed to have our guards up. The point I should have listened to those doubts prodding at my brain and not just walked stupidly into the next challenge.

Did you ever see such a thing in your life . . .

And I get stuck. Because Naira's maze was uncomfortable, but we didn't see anything to make us suspect it wasn't a standard part of the escape room. Gus and Hal's electric shocks were bad, but not life-threatening. This game is on another level.

As three blind mice.

The lights turn green. The pressure on my shoulders eases as the walls move back to their original positions and the door swings open. I step out of the box, taking in a huge gulp of not-box air, and my legs feel shaky but I need to check on the others.

Colette is off her stool and trying to brush the spiders off Naira while Hallie and Gus, both dripping – Hal with water and Gus with blood-red something – try to get the worst of the liquid off themselves and out of their clothes. My box was horrible, but at least I have no reminders of it crawling over me or trickling down my face.

'It'll be easier to get them off if you can stand still, Naira,' I say, holding her hands. Her face is practically grey, her eyes scrunched shut. But she nods and forces herself to stop thrashing around, although she's still trembling hard. Then Col and I brush the spiders off her. And as far as I can see there's nothing mutated or unnatural about them – they're just normal house and garden spiders. And I know that doesn't matter when you have a fear of something, but at least it means that if any of them bit her, there shouldn't be any serious damage.

'I'm so sorry.' Colette is crying.

'Nothing to be sorry for,' Naira says through chattering teeth.

'Yeah, Col.' Hallie comes to help with the

spider flicking. She's totally soaked up to her shoulders. She looks shaken but also crazy angry. 'This was not your fault.'

'You did brilliantly,' I say, squeezing her hand. 'Look, we're all out and none of us are hurt.'

'Maybe not physically,' Colette says. 'But I'm pretty sure you're all going to be emotionally scarred for life.'

'We were anyway.' Gus has taken off his hoodie and used the inside of it to wipe the red off his face, which is good in a way but it shows up the green tinge to his skin. 'So it's no big thing.'

'How many times did you puke?' Colette says.

'Enough to see literally everything I ate at Uccellino's.' Gus makes a face. 'But at least it means I'll get a bit longer before my stoma bag needs changing.'

'Oh god.' Colette rubs her puffy eyes. 'This was supposed to be fun.'

The last of the spiders has hurried away into a dark corner and Naira finally opens her eyes. The first thing she does is look at the countdown clock. Ten minutes remaining.

'How were we only in there for seven minutes?' she gasps. 'It felt like forever.'

'So what now?' I say. 'We only have ten minutes left to escape. And I don't know what the bigger plan is here . . .'

'. . . 'Cos someone Latchitt-related is clearly messing with us,' Hallie says.

'I mean, they put spiders in with Naira, which they know she hates . . .' Hallie says.

'And trapped Hallie in a sinking-ship-type situation, like on our school trip . . .' Naira says.

'And sprayed Gus with blood, like we did to them when we got the vampire birds to burst the blood balloons,' Colette says. She's stopped crying but she looks wrecked.

'And they trapped us in a toilet cubicle while we were playing Flinch,' Hallie says. 'Which feels like about a thousand years ago.'

'If this is the Latchitts then we need to leave,' Colette says. But the only doors are the one we came in through, which is locked, and the exit.

I sigh. 'We're under their control now. We can't go back so we'll check out the next room. If it looks dangerous we'll find another way out.'

'The only way out is through,' Gus says, and he turns towards the exit. 'That's what they told us. So far the Latchitts, if it is the Latchitts, have stuck to the rules of the games. They could have shut us in at any point. They could have hurt us . . .'

'. . . But they didn't,' Colette says. 'They've allowed us to continue. Maybe 'cos they have something even worse planned . . .'

'Oh, for scrut's sake,' Hallie says. 'As long as you know, I'm going to lose *all* of my shiz once we're out of here.'

'We would expect no less from you, Halster,' Gus says.

We push through the exit door into what we hope is the final room.

It looks a lot like the first room. An office, with a desk and a computer. Nothing stands out as being likely to crush, pound or dismember us. As expected, the doors are firmly shut, and nothing we do to them makes them move, even the smallest amount. So we all gather round the computer screen to read the instructions:

PHOTO-FIT: In the desk drawer, you will find the pieces of a puzzle that you must assemble on this desk. There is one piece missing. This can only be obtained by solving a clue. Once the final piece of the puzzle has been won and placed correctly, the exit door will open.

We pull the puzzle pieces out of the drawer and start flipping them over. We're all shaky, and conscious of the seconds ticking down. It feels like the stakes are much higher now than they were when we walked into the Project Z reception area an hour ago. Naira separates the corners and edges.

'Let me place the pieces,' she says, her hands moving like lightning across the desk. 'If we all try to do it at the same time, we'll get in each other's way. Tell me if you see where something needs to go, and I'll do it.'

So we watch, mostly in silence, while she arranges the pieces. And as the puzzle begins to come together, that familiar twisting of dread pulls at my stomach.

'So this is a picture of us, right?' Colette says, as Naira moves more pieces into place.

'A picture of us from earlier,' Hallie says. 'One of the selfies we took by the Battle Karts.'

'Do you still have your phone, Hal?' I say.

'Yep.' She holds it up. 'I've had it with me the whole time, I'm certain. And if nobody's had my phone they must have hacked the cloud to get it.' She starts scrolling through her photo feed. I look over her shoulder at all the goofy photos from our time in the Perch. Feels like days ago.

Hal looks down at the almost complete puzzle picture on the desk. 'But this photo's not here, and it definitely was earlier. I remember flicking through them and thinking it was a good one because all of us were making derpy faces but without looking like bog trolls. It was a keeper. How could it be deleted from my phone?'

'That's it.' Naira looks up from the puzzle. 'We've used all the pieces.'

The computer screen flickers and a new message appears:

To win the final piece of the puzzle and escape from the room, you must solve the following clue: Arrange the first letters of your names into a word and type it in the space below. One of your names should behave as it suggests.

Then a series of dashes pop up in a line, one by one.

'There are seven,' Colette says. 'Seven letters, but only five of us.'

'Ninety seconds left on the clock,' I say.

'So we have H, G, N, A and C.' Hallie counts the letters off on her fingers. 'Which is only five so that doesn't make sense.'

'What can we spell with them?' Gus says. 'I can only think of *CHANG* or *GANCH*.'

'*GANCH* is not a word,' Naira says. 'And I don't see how *CHANG* is relevant.'

'Hold up,' I say. 'We're not supposed to use our real names in this game, so maybe it means our code names.'

'Yes, Angelo!' Colette says. 'So E, R, G, N, V. But they don't spell anything.'

'Remember there are seven spaces, so we might need to use some of them more than once,' Naira says.

'Most likely the vowel.' My brain is trying hard to focus on the letters rather than the clock, but I'm getting nothing.

'Yes, Angelo!' Naira gasps. 'It's the E! Behaves as it suggests – echo!'

'Echo, echo,' Gus whispers.

'So . . .' Colette says, and we all fall silent for a few seconds, the concentration in the room so focused that it feels like the whole place could combust.

'I got it!' Hallie leans over Naira and types on the computer keyboard: R, E, V, E, N, G, E.

'Of course it is,' Naira says. 'How could it be anything else?'

And I allow myself one, two seconds to try to take it in, but it's not enough time and the clock is still ticking.

'Where's the missing puzzle piece?' Colette starts looking around. 'There should be a hatch or something?'

We start pulling at the desk drawers. Thirty-two seconds on the clock.

'Message!' Gus yells, pointing at the monitor. Then he reads, '*The final piece of the puzzle is with the birthday girl.*'

We all look at Colette who looks like she might be sick.

'Where?' she gasps and she starts turning her

pockets inside out, sending bits of fluff and tissue, arcade tokens and coins, flying across the room. Then she rips off her jumper, turning it inside out and shaking it, and my eyes fall on her Project Z security ID which has come unclipped and dropped to the floor. The one thing she has that she didn't arrive here with. I pick it up and wriggle the badge out of the plastic holder. My hands are sweating and I know there can only be about ten seconds left of the game. But then the badge unfolds, a puzzle piece drops out, and I slam it into the hole in the jigsaw without even looking at it. It's only when it's in place and the room is lit green that I get to see on the photo what we didn't see when we were taking it.

We all stand around the puzzle, the colours distorted by the green glow, but the image crystal clear, too shocked to speak. Because while we were posing and laughing, full of adrenaline and excitement for the night ahead. Looking into the camera like idiots who've got out of their car on a safari and are just about to be attacked by lions. Standing behind us, a way back, but unmistakeably there – even though we thought they couldn't possibly be there – smiling nastily at the camera are two people who send a bolt of fear through my entire body.

The Latchitts.

CHAPTER TEN

THE REAL GAME BEGINS

'We should leave now,' Colette says, picking her jumper off the floor. She looks so sad. Not just from crying in Powerplay, but defeated. Like she's resigned herself to the Latchitts ruining her life.

'Whatever's on the other side of that door, we'll be OK,' I say, holding her hand. 'We've beaten them before.'

'Multiple times,' Naira says.

'And remember that Hallie has promised to lose, not just some, but all of her shiz,' Gus says. 'That's a lot.'

'Hell yeah,' Hallie says, cracking her knuckles. 'I am so ready to unleash everything I have on those creeps.'

'Speaking of shiz,' Naira says, taking a deep sniff of her top. 'Do we all smell really bad? I feel like we do.'

Gus raises his hand. 'I bet I smell the worst. Stinking gas jets, rotten blood spray and eau de puke. Triple threat.'

'The water they tried to drown me in reeked too,' Hallie says. 'Same kind of smell as the smoke they kept blasting at us.'

I shrug. 'At least we all stink together.'

'Club Loser for the win,' Gus says.

Then we push open the door.

Beyond it there's a short corridor that leads back to somewhere we've been before.

'The lift of doom,' Gus groans. 'It's like

we've run around in a big circle and all we have to show for it is dirty clothes, tingling nerve endings and a lifetime's worth of emotional trauma.'

'Welcome to the final game, sweetlings.' Mrs Latchitt's voice surrounds us, creaking out of some hidden speaker. The sound of it is so horrifying that it almost physically hurts – prickling over my body like someone's just thrown a bucket of balled-up hedgehogs at me.

'And we'd like to wish our estranged granddaughter a memorable thirteenth birthday.' She giggles. 'What a joy it is to be able to reunite for the celebrations.'

We've all stopped still and are looking around us, ready for an attack of some kind.

'You think they can see and hear us?' Colette says.

'I'm sure they're watching on the CCTV,' I say, noticing a camera in the corner of the ceiling above the lift. 'But I don't know if they can hear.'

'Every birthday party needs games, sweetlings,' Mrs Latchitt carries on.

'And thanks to you we've had time to plan something extra special,' Mr Latchitt growls.

'I thought people who went to prison did wholesome things, like learning to sew or bake,' Gus says. 'Just our luck that these guys decided to spend their days planning extreme and whimsical revenge.'

'And why are they out of prison?' Naira says. 'The CPS said the case against them was . . .'

'Robust,' Hallie sighs.

'Something must have gone wrong,' Colette said. 'And no one thought to tell us they're roaming the streets again like mangy cats.'

'We're sure you have many questions, sweetlings,' Mrs Latchitt says.

'Maybe they *are* listening,' Hallie says.

'Could be reading our lips,' I say, 'cos I'm not convinced.

'Or our minds,' Gus whispers.

'But we have one final game to play.' Mrs

Latchitt giggles again. 'And this time you'll have the run of the entire building.'

'It's a battle of wits,' Mr Latchitt says. 'The five of you against some loyal members of our tribe.'

I try not to react, not wanting them to see my fear.

'And when they're victorious, we will show the world that we are unbeatable,' Mrs Latchitt says. 'And you, little mice, will be dead.'

My mouth is muesli-straight-out-of-the-packet dry. My heart is punching me from the inside like it wants to shatter my ribcage. But I try to keep my face empty. The Latchitts get a kick out of scaring us and I'm not having it this time.

'Your task is simple . . .' Mr Latchitt says.

'So cute the way they take turns to speak,' Gus whispers. 'Still going strong with the couple goals, even after months in different cells.'

'. . . This building has been cleared of people,

and is locked up tight. All you need to do is defeat your opponents and free yourselves.'

'Then you can flee the Perch and fly away home,' Mrs Latchitt says.

'You might ask why you should even play,' Mr Latchitt's voice snarls, so low and rumbly that I swear the walls are vibrating.

'I bet the sly little fox is already thinking up tricks in his wily brain,' Mrs Latchitt hisses. 'He suspects that we're putting him in a race he can't win. Why not huddle down in his burrow and wait for help to arrive?'

I mean, there's no way I was going to huddle down and wait for help, but sure, I wasn't planning to do what they say either.

'So we planned an extra treat for you,' Mrs Latchitt squeals. 'A generous bonus to sweeten the deal.'

'I hope it's cash,' I say. ''Cos that's the only thing I might consider.'

'Or a pet T-Rex,' Gus says. ''Cos I'm pretty sure they could actually do that.'

'I'd rather have a triceratops,' Hallie says.

'That's because you *are* a triceratops,' Gus snorts. 'You only eat leaves and you like headbutting things.'

'Diplodocus for me,' Colette says. 'I'd ride it to school. What about you, Nai?'

'I really don't want a dinosaur. But I'd take the cash.'

'OK, so cash or dinosaurs are the only bonuses we'll consider,' I say to the closest camera. Partly because I want to know if they can hear us or not. If they can't then that's definitely something we can use.

'Turn to the screen on the door you just came through.' Mr Latchitt sounds like he's getting annoyed, but I notice he hasn't referenced any of the specific things we've said through this whole weird tannoy conversation.

We turn to see another one of those ancient iPads behind us showing a series of black and white images that flick from one to the next every few seconds. We stare at them in silence, trying to work out what we're looking at.

'Isn't that school?' Naira says.

'Yeah.' My eyes move from screen to screen, piecing the images together. I can see the main entrance and the foyer, with people standing around in pairs and small groups, chatting and laughing. There's a table set up with tea and coffee urns and plates of biscuits. And on the next screen there's a view of the school hall from above. Chairs are set out in rows facing the stage, where Mr Hume's podium looms over everything. 'It's the meeting Mr C told us about.'

'The meeting that our parents are at,' Gus sighs.

I scan the next couple of screens showing different angles of the hall. I can see parents moving down the rows of seats, removing coats, unravelling scarves and looking through booklets that have been placed on each chair.

'Oh god,' Colette says. 'Look, Raph is there too.'

And I see that she's right. My heart sinks as I watch my dad taking a seat in the hall with Raph next to him, reading one of his space books.

'It's a live stream of the meeting at school,' Hallie says.

'We have some surprise guests ready to release into the hall,' Mr Latchitt says. 'All it will take is the push of a button to create carnage. So here's your incentive: if you finish the game, we won't destroy your loved ones.'

CHAPTER ELEVEN

BREAKING IN AND BREAKING OUT

I feel sick.

The Latchitts know Dread Wood High inside out, and we all know what they're capable of. It's completely possible that they've hidden some murderous creature at the school and would happily set it loose on a bunch of totally innocent people. Hell, it's not even possible, it's straight out of their evil playbook.

We stare at the screens. This changes everything.

'You'd think going to one of Mr Hume's meetings would be punishment enough.' Gus sighs, and I can see both his parents there, waving at my dad and walking towards the row he's on to sit with him. 'But they just had to take it to the next level.'

'So we're playing, right?' Naira says, her eyes fixed on her mum who, in a very Naira-like way, is focused on reading all the information in the booklet. 'At least . . .' She stops herself, rubs her nose to cover her mouth while she whispers, 'At least while we figure something out.'

'We have to.' Hallie nods.

'Yeah,' Colette says.

So I turn to look at the camera again, staring into it as if I can see the Latchitts, wherever they're hiding, staring back at me. And I nod.

'You have an hour,' Mr Latchitt says. 'If you aren't out by then, you aren't coming out at all.'

The screen changes to a new countdown clock. Sixty minutes and counting.

'Let the game begin,' Mrs Latchitt says. 'Off you scamper, little blind mice, let us see how you run.'

There's a click as the tannoy switches off, and then silence.

'Back in the lift then,' I say, pressing the up button.

'So what are we thinking?' Hallie says, as we wait for the lift as it whirrs towards us. 'One big monster or multiple small monsters?'

'I don't think you've stopped to consider multiple big monsters.' Colette looks back down the corridor behind us. Scanning for signs of life.

'If it's whatever was with us before, which seems probable, then it's small,' Naira says. 'But size won't really matter if there are hundreds of them.'

'Or if they have superpowers,' Gus says.

I pull my phone out of my pocket, check for

a non-existent signal, and turn the torch on. 'If something, or someone, joins us in this lift, I'm going to make sure I can at least see them this time.' Because now I'm thinking maybe it *was* Mrs Latchitt in the lift with us earlier. Although that wouldn't explain how I was holding a hand that felt the same as Colette's, or saw someone who looked like Colette.

The lift pings, and I brace myself as the doors slide open. But the lift is . . .

'Empty!' Gus says. 'I'm almost disappointed. Now it just feels like we're in a department store and my mum is making us go to the fourth floor to look at homeware.'

We walk in and press the button to take us back up to the non-zombie world.

'I wonder what we'll find up there,' Naira says, as the doors close and the lift starts to move.

'Bed covers, frying pans, an unnecessary array of cushions, that sort of thing,' Gus says. 'It is the most boring floor.'

And despite the fear gnawing away at my gut like a half-starved rodent, I let out a snort of laughter.

Naira sighs and continues like Gus never said anything. 'I wonder how they cleared the building?'

'Probably murdered everyone and threw them in the car park,' Colette says. 'The ground is strewn with bodies and half-eaten tacos.'

'Sometimes you're surprisingly dark, Col,' Hallie says, in a way like she really respects it.

Then the lift jerks to a stop at the same time as a blast of disgusting-smelling smoke spurts out of a device on the ceiling, covering us in grey powdery rankness.

It catches in my throat, making me cough and choke, and then gag on the vile taste of it. Clearly something bad is about to happen and we need to get out of this lift.

'We're between floors, right?' I say.

Gus starts pounding the button with his fist,

but the lights on the display flicker off and the control panel doesn't respond.

'Seems like we're stuck here then,' Hallie says.

'But stuck here on purpose because the Latchitts planned it this way? Or stuck here due to some faulty electrics?' Gus is pressing the up button in a bunch of different ways – really gently and slowly, multiple times rapidly, a surprise press where he makes out he's given up and then suddenly launches at it.

'Are you trying to trick the lift into working, Gustav?' Naira asks.

'Sshhh, Nai-Nai,' Gus whispers. 'Don't give the game away – it might be listening.'

And then we all freeze as an unmistakeable scratching sound comes from below the floor of the lift, accompanied by a chittering noise that sends shivers down my spine.

'Sounds like claws scraping the metal,' Colette whispers. We're all staring at the area around our feet like we've just realised we're standing in quicksand.

A piercing shriek cuts through the scratching, like someone's dragging a knife across the steel. 'Also maybe teeth,' I say. I notice a slight ridge in the metal in one of the corners of the floor. And then with another squeal of blade on metal, a second one rises up, like a swollen scratch across skin.

'There's more than one of them, and they're going to get inside,' Naira says. 'Which means we need to find a way out.'

'Anyone got anything to prise the doors open with?' Gus says, unzipping kitty and looking inside, like the perfect tool for the job might somehow be in there. 'What we need is a pointy stick.'

'What we need is a crowbar,' Hallie says. She tries to grip the edges of the doors and pull them back, but her fingers just slide off. 'And sadly I didn't bring mine with me today.'

'Forget the doors,' I say, looking around for alternatives as the bottom of the lift continues to be ravaged. 'We're between floors anyway, so there will probably just be a wall behind them.' There's only one option. 'We have to go up.'

'Boost me,' Naira says to Gus, and he kneels down and links his hands together to launch her up to the ceiling, which is made up of a grid of metal squares. She pushes on it in a few places until one of them moves. Then she hammers it with the palm of her hand, making it creak and rattle.

'Go on, Nai-Nai,' Gus whoops.

A moment later the metal plate pops upwards, leaving a gap that we should be able to squeeze through.

Naira puts her head through to look around. 'All clear,' she shouts. 'And there's a ladder we can climb up.'

It's great we have a way out but . . .

'Seems too easy,' Colette says, as Naira pulls herself through the gap and on to the top of the lift.

'Yeah,' I nod. 'But it's all we can do, right?' I kneel down to boost her up while Naira grabs her wrists and helps her from above.

The creaking, chittering and scraping noises are getting louder, and an area of the floor is starting to buckle. We don't have long until whatever is down there breaks through. Hallie goes up next, then Gus. I take one last look at the slash-covered floor before I jump to grab the hands waiting to help me up. There's a split in the metal. And through it I can see the glint of an eye – somehow dark and red and bright at the same time, like a burning coal – looking at me like I'm its dinner.

CHAPTER TWELVE

CREEPY CRAWL

The lift shaft is as dark, dirty and claustrophobic as you'd expect. Machinery coated in black grime, and thick cables shining dully from pulling the lift up and down every day. The air smells of grease and old cobwebs. The others are already climbing the ladder like they're being chased by Vecna, their hands and feet clanging against the rungs – Hallie first, followed by Gus and Col.

'I don't think I've ever seen them move so fast,' I say to Naira, as she pulls me to my feet.

'Fear of death by lift squishing can do that to a person,' she says. 'You know, just in case it starts working again and carries on moving upwards.'

'Jesus,' I say, because that would be truly pants-ruining scary. 'Go on,' I say, pushing Naira towards the ladder. 'I'm right behind you.'

I wait while she springs like an athlete up the first few rungs, then I grab the ladder and climb as fast as I can, hoping my sweaty hands won't slip and send me tumbling back down.

'Problem, gang,' Hallie yells. 'I've reached the doors for the next floor, but it's the same sitch as in the lift – I can't open them.'

'We need to find another way out,' Naira yells. 'There must be other access tunnels, or ventilation grates. Keep looking.'

We climb for another few metres, and I'm trying not to picture the lift hurtling towards us, or the hungry-eyed creature making it out of the lift and on to the ladder. And then Hallie shouts again. 'Found a loose ventilation grate. Not sure where it will take us but at least we'll be out of the lift shaft. I just need to kick it in.'

The thuds and clangs of Hallie beating the hell out of the grate echo around the shaft, and I'm showered in falling dust and grit. I close my eyes. Try not to breathe it in. And then a large sheet of metal plunges down the lift shaft to the right of the ladder, clattering on to the top of the lift. From the height of the opening in relation to the doors we passed, I think it's taking us into the ceiling above the first floor.

'We're in!' Hallie shouts, and I wait while she, Gus, Col and then Nai disappear into the black. I follow, and almost wish I hadn't. We're in a narrow space, balancing on a rough wooden beam only wide enough for single file, and the space is only tall enough for us to crawl through. I instantly feel the walls of pipes and boxed-in cabling close in around me. The dark. The dirt. The weird stuffy smell. The others have switched their phone lights on, and the beams swing and wobble in a dizzying way that makes me want to close my eyes and curl in a ball. But instead I look around. There's no visible way out of this cramped-up maze, other than back the way we came, and the path ahead is full of shadows. I hope we're not going to regret this.

'Still no way of contacting the outside world?' I ask.

'No signal. No Wi-Fi,' Gus says, checking his phone. 'Nada. The signal must be being blocked.'

'Let's get moving then,' I sigh.

'We want to head in this direction, right?' Hallie waves her light towards where the centre of what I think must be the first floor would be, way below us. I have no clue how we're going to get down. But my thoughts are interrupted by a scuffling sound below, like something's climbing up after us.

'Right,' I yell. 'Go.'

And she starts crawling up the widest metal beam, the light from her torch swaying as she places her hands, one after the other, in front of her. The others follow.

I'm tight behind Naira as she crawls, my face level with her butt, hoping that Hallie can pick her way through the maze even though she's terrible at finding her way anywhere. I remember when we were stuck on the *Melusine* and she'd literally take the same wrong corridor five times in a row.

'Crossroads coming up,' Hallie shouts. 'Turning left.'

A minute later, I see Naira turning sharply left in front of me. So I follow, wishing there was enough space to stand up. This would be so much less awful if I could stand up.

'Dead end!' Hallie shouts. 'Reverse!'

So we crawl backwards, bumping into each

other, Naira's butt in my face, our knees crunching against the hard surfaces below us. It's clumsy as hell, and takes much longer than I'd like, but we have no other choice. When I get back to the intersection, I take the right turn.

I move forward, shining my torch ahead of me to illuminate a long, straight passage formed by clusters of pipes that snake off in every direction. They connect together in huge boxes made of metal sheeting, and in some places form complex tangles with the ropes of cabling. The passage is a little wider than the previous one, although not enough to make it any less uncomfortable, and it has multiple openings on each side that could lead to other routes or just dead ends. I crawl as fast as I can, taking a quick look at each of the openings but trying not to stop or slow down as I do so.

'Everyone still behind me?' I say, as quietly as I can while still loud enough to be heard. Who knows where the Latchitts are right now.

'Present and correct,' Naira says.

'Peachy.' I hear Colette's voice. She sounds OK, considering.

'Affirmative,' Gus calls from behind.

'Having the time of my life,' Hallie yells from way back. 'No sign of demonic creatures in pursuit.'

And I allow myself half a second of feeling grateful that we're all still here. Still in one piece. No serious injuries. Still able to fight when we need to – and I'm sure we'll need to. Though I wish we knew exactly what kind of animal we're going to be dealing with.

My back is aching with the desperate need to stand up or stretch out and I feel my pulse quicken, my breathing get harder. Sweat is tickling the skin around my hairline and I have the urge to scratch it so hard that it makes me bleed. I'm panicking. I bite my lip. Try not to think about it. *Focus, Angelo.* Three quarters of the way up the tunnel and there's a large opening on the left.

I shine my phone light into it and am distracted away from the crippling claustrophobia. I stop crawling and this time Naira's head bumps into my butt.

'Little warning next time?' she says. But then I hear an 'oof' as Colette bumps into her, and the others carry it on down the line like dominoes.

'Sorry,' I say. 'We're turning left. I think it's a bit lighter this way, so it might be a way back down into the Perch.'

'Oh really?' Hallie says. 'That's a shame because I'm having so much fun cockroaching around in this hellscape.'

I twist my back to make the sharp left turn.

'Wait.' Naira puts her hand on my ankle suddenly. Gripping it firmly, stopping me from crawling forward.

I freeze instantly. I know from her voice and the tension in her hand on my ankle that something's wrong. The others must feel it too, because everyone falls silent.

'Where?' I whisper.

'Not sure,' Naira whispers back. 'But there's something.'

My eyes are stinging from the constant onslaught of dust and grit flying up around us. But I open them wide and look around me, beyond the yellow beams from our phone lights, into the shadows. I count the seconds in my head: one, two, three . . . and my eyeballs are burning now. Tear droplets form along the lower eyelids and start to roll down my face, joining the trickles of sweat in a hot salty mess. Maybe the creatures from the lift have made it into the roof space. But I can't see any movement in the tunnels around us. Not yet anyway.

And then I hear it: rhythmic, repetitive. Soft thuds and scrapes. The sound of something moving along the beams just as we are. And that's the part that makes my skin prickle with goosebumps, and my blood – pumping hotly through my body just a minute ago – feels like ice inside me. Because it's not like the scratching we heard earlier. Whatever's up here with us is bigger. Human.

'Which way?' Hallie whispers.

'It's hard to work out,' Naira says. 'Because of the echoes. Everything is distorted.'

My body tenses, ready to crawl like my life depends on it. I'm desperate to stand up and run, and for a second I feel overwhelmed by the coffin vibes of this god-awful crawl space. If I make it out of here, I am never coming up again. Ever.

The thump and drag of whoever's stalking us is getting louder so I concentrate on locating it. There's a change of direction as they turn a corner and then it's suddenly horribly close.

I raise my phone light, my hand shaking in an annoyingly unhelpful way, and sweep it in a slow circle around me. Pipes. Cables. Steel boxes with cooling vents. A twisted maze covered in grime.

And then I shine it down the tunnel to my

left. The tunnel that was going to lead us to freedom. And I can finally see what's coming for us. Wild curly hair, as grey as the blanket of dust around us, gleams silver in the torchlight. And in the middle of it all, a face grins at me. Old and wrinkled, but full of vengeful energy. Eyes shining with joy, or rage, or stone-cold cruelty, looking at me like I'm a treat she wants to devour.

'Peekaboo, sweetlings,' Mrs Latchitt says. 'I've come to join in the game.'

CHAPTER THIRTEEN

RATS IN A MAZE

The rush of horror that tsunamis through me is so powerful that everything else becomes a blur. I jerk backwards, smashing into Naira again, but hard this time. My knee crushes her hand, and she gasps in pain. I don't even have a second to apologise, because every single part of me is focused on getting all of us away. The ghosts of screams echo around the ceiling maze, and I realise that although the others can't see Mrs Latchitt from where they're positioned, they definitely heard her. I try to turn my head to see Colette, Gus and Hal, but my view is blocked by Naira who's already pushing me forward, away from the turning and further up the passage.

The stuffy air is filled with dust motes and panic as we scrabble around in the dirt, trying to put some distance between us and Mrs Latchitt who is moving up the tunnel towards us, cackling like a witch. 'Hide-and-seek, is it, sweetlings?' she says. 'Or how about a game of tag? Off you scurry, little mice. And I will catch you.'

I can only go forward. So I crawl, as fast as I can, feeling my clothes tear as they catch on splinters and sharp corners.

'We're not going to make it that way,' Colette yells out from way behind Naira, and I panic, realising there's a huge gap between us. Naira and I both turn to look back down the passage where I can just see a glimpse of Colette, Gus and Hallie heading in the opposite direction. 'We'll find you!' Colette shouts, and then they're gone. Crawling back the way we came.

I want to scream. I want to go after them. But Mrs Latchitt emerges from her tunnel, halfway between us and them, and I know the best thing we can do is try to lead her away. She looks in both directions, her face lit up like a five-year-old on Christmas morning.

'Hmm, the mice have scattered,' she says. And I want to get the hell away from her, but even more than that I want her to get the hell away from Colette. So I force myself to wait, hoping the fact that we're closer will be enough to lure her towards us.

Mrs Latchitt pulls herself out of the tunnel so that she's fully in our stretch of the maze now. So horribly close. She sits back on her heels and lifts a gnarly finger, pointing it at the other end of the tunnel where Col, Gus and Hal have turned off.

'*Eeny*,' she says. Then she points at us.

'*Meeny*.' Her fingernails are long and dirty and they make me feel sick. '*Miny*.' She points the opposite way again.

And I'm pretty sure I know where this is going, but still I hesitate, wanting to make sure. I feel Naira tense beside me, ready to crawl.

'*Moe!*' Mrs Latchitt points her horrible finger at us one more time, and fires up the passageway faster than you'd think possible. So now we don't wait. We go. Crawling, crawling, crawling. Scraping our knees and whacking our elbows. Choking on dust, the dead-skin smell of it filling our noses. And I'm feeling this terrible responsibility because I'm in front. It's not me she'll get to first, it's Naira. I can't mess up. I can't slip, or fall, or lead us down a dead end. At the end of the tunnel, I turn left, but only for a short way because it opens out into a wider space, with five different tunnels leading off like the spokes of a wheel.

I don't have time to think it through so I go

with my gut and plunge into the second passage on the left, feeling Naira right on my heels, her breathing fast. This tunnel is narrower. In parts so close that we have to angle our bodies to squeeze through. My head is pounding with the thought that I've taken us the wrong way. That we're going to end up in a gap so small that we get stuck and have to remain there, waiting for either Mrs Latchitt or the mystery creatures to finish us off.

'Hold up,' Naira gasps. 'She's not behind us any more.'

So I stop, and I listen, and Naira's right. The bumping of Mrs Latchitt's hands and knees against the beams has stopped. There's no scuffling. And no giggling.

'You think she's gone after the others?' I say.

'I don't know, but if she has there's nothing we can do about it,' Naira says. 'The best thing we can do is carry on and find a way . . .'

A bony hand reaches out of the darkness to my right and grips on to my arm with fingers like vices, the nails cutting into my skin.

'Got you, sweetling.' Mrs Latchitt's face appears from the shadows. 'Now what will I do with you? Perhaps I should cut off your tail?'

I yell and jerk backwards, whacking my head on a pipe and feeling the crunch of it jolting through my entire body. But Mrs Latchitt doesn't let go.

I can't kick out because of the cramped space and my feet being trapped beneath me at the wrong angle. So all I have is my other arm to fight her with. I drop my phone and grab Mrs Latchitt's hand, trying to prise it off my wrist. I pull and twist, but it's like her bones are made of iron.

'Don't give up, Angelo,' Naira yells behind me.

'Oh, but you will,' Mrs Latchitt says. 'You all will, sweetlings. There can only be one ending to our tale and it's not going to be happily ever after for you. Nobody wants to see the treacherous villains win.'

'You think we're the villains?' I gasp, letting go of her hand because even using all of my strength, it's not shifting.

Mrs Latchitt laughs. 'Did you think you were the heroes, sweetling? After everything you've done?'

And I'm shocked, just for a second or two, because it's never occurred to me that the Latchitts think they're the good guys. I mean, they're clearly evil. At least I've always thought so. I assumed they knew, like how I know my eyes are brown and I'm left-handed. It's just facts.

Mrs Latchitt slides forward, at the same time pulling me towards her like she's reeling in a fish for her dinner.

'Take a look in the mirror, wily fox.' She grins. 'You're a thief and a liar. You scuttle around at the edges of your world, slinking, sneaking, hunting for scraps. You ignore the rules and defy those who seek to put you on the right path.'

Part of my brain is screaming at me to ignore her – to let those words slip down to the ground to be trampled on and forgotten. But the other part of my brain is letting them in. Questioning and doubting.

'That's total scrut, you vicious old hag,' Naira yells. And the shock of hearing her curse and name-call brings me back to the moment. 'Don't listen to her, Angelo. She's deranged.'

'Deranged, am I?' Mrs Latchitt hisses.

'Yeah, that's what I said,' Naira snaps back. 'You do realise that, right? Deranged, unhinged, moral code all over the place . . .'

I know she's trying to keep Mrs Latchitt talking – Mrs Latchitt loves talking – so we can think of a way out of this.

'My moral code is impeccable,' Mrs Latchitt says. She's focusing more on Naira than she is on gripping my arm. 'Family, loyalty, devotion to the pursuit of knowledge that will benefit the human race . . .'

'By abusing animals and carrying out illegal

experiments,' Naira says. 'And then using the results of those experiments to hurt innocent people.'

'There are no innocent people,' Mrs Latchitt snarls. 'We are creating a better world.'

'You're selling monsters for money,' Naira says. 'There's nothing good or honourable in that.'

I try to focus. Mrs Latchitt is distracted and we can use that. If I can get free of her, we could crawl away.

'We're growing our family,' Mrs Latchitt says. 'And helping others to grow theirs. We need funding to continue our work and there are many who are glad to donate it.'

'You wouldn't need to grow your family if you hadn't made your own daughter hate you,' Naira says.

But could we crawl fast enough? Ma Latchitt is crazy fast and seems to know her way around this maze of passages, so she'll either catch us or cut us off in another tunnel. What we need is the element of surprise – to do something she's not expecting. I glance at the surfaces on either side of the beam we're balancing on. They look like ceiling tiles – flimsy enough to break without too much effort.

'Our daughter was a cuckoo in the nest.' Mrs Latchitt's narrowed eyes are gazing over my shoulder, fixed on Naira. 'Not every creation is a success. Trial and error, test after test, until you achieve the results you're striving for: that is the nature of science.'

I have an idea. It's risky. But I can't think of another way.

'And that ungrateful granddaughter,' Mrs Latchitt carries on, clearly on a rant now that Nai's got her talking about her favourite subject. 'We did what we could for her, tried to bring her into the fold. Out of kindness and familial duty.'

'You mean you stalked her and tried to murder people in her name, even though she would never want you to do that?' Naira says.

I brace myself for what I need to do next.

'We guarded her,' Mrs Latchitt hisses. 'We protected her. And how does she show her gratitude? By taking away our only son.'

'Your son died because he got in a boat with a load of poisonous octopuses,' Naira says. 'Death by stupidity.'

Mrs Latchitt is so furious that I can practically see the anger steaming off her like a demon burning up in daylight. She glares at Naira, snarling like a rabid wolf, and I know there won't be a better moment than this. I lean forward and sink my teeth into her hand, biting as hard as I can. Trying to ignore the feel of her leathery skin against my lips, and the taste of evil old lady, I increase the pressure until she lets go with a furious scream. Then I rock backwards with as much momentum as I can. I grab Naira and pull both of us off the beam so that we crash on to the ceiling tiles running alongside it. There's a second where I think my plan has failed – that the tiles are going to hold and we'll have to face Mrs Latchitt in full Hulk mode. But then there's a crack as the tiles buckle under our weight. Then another as they sag downwards, holding on by a few fibres before giving way completely.

I squeeze my eyes shut against the sudden rush of bright light that blinds me as we plummet from the ceiling towards the ground below.

CHAPTER FOURTEEN

BLOOD AND SKIN

I'm aware of Mrs Latchitt shrieking with rage, and Naira screaming in shock and fear as we drop like over-ripe apples from a tree. My body is stiff with tension, and I just have time to relax it – unlocking my knees and bending all my joints slightly – before impact. I curl my arms around my head to protect it, knowing – or at least hoping – that Naira will be doing the same.

The impact hits before I expect it to, my feet smashing into something hard at what I feel like is only the halfway point of the drop. The force of it thunderbolts through my entire skeleton, making my jaw smash shut and my mouth fill with blood.

And then my lower back bounces on to whatever surface I'm landing on, and I half bounce and half slide downwards like I'm on a slope. I try to tuck myself in so I can roll instead of scraping most of my skin off, but it's so fast, and my brain is pinging off the inside of my skull like a trapped bee against a window, and I know it's all too little, too late.

I manage to half open my eyes as the gradient of the slope becomes less steep, and my fall less fast and less violent. I look for Naira and see her, just a metre or so away from me, rolling too. But of course doing it more gracefully than I am, because it's Nai, and even when she's falling she's doing it better than anyone else. And I'm so relieved. And then relieved again as my battered body reaches flat ground at last and I come to a stop.

I lie there for a second, trying to get my breath back. Trying not to think about all the places where pain is slicing through my skin and bones.

'You OK, Nai?' I gasp.

'Sorta,' she says, through fast breaths. 'Lucky we hit the volcano.'

I turn my head to the side and look at the craggy slope of Olympus Mons rising up out of the ground next to me, the centrepiece of the Galactic Golf course on the first floor of the Neon Perch, close to where we were eating in Uccellino's less than two hours ago. Its rough, rust-coloured surface is now covered in a good layer of my skin. Nai's too probably.

'Yeah. And lucky it's a volcano on the Red Planet so our blood doesn't show up too much,' I say. 'Don't want to scare the kids at their mini-golf birthday parties.'

I heave myself into a sitting position and

squint at the hole in the ceiling above us. Mrs Latchitt has gone. But that doesn't mean we're safe.

'Can you get up?' I ask.

'Yep.' Naira gets to her feet, testing each leg, flexing her arms. She doesn't seem to have done any serious damage at least. 'You?'

I stand up too. It hurts like a raging beast from hell, but nothing gives way. 'Apparently I can.'

'It looks strange in here,' Naira says, gazing at the empty area around us. 'You'd think having the Neon Perch to yourself would be fun.'

The Perch is deserted, but the lights are still on and I can hear the distant beeping of arcade machines. The screens in Galactic Golf display the scores of half-played games, and illuminated signs point the way to VR Gaming, Songbirds Karaoke and downstairs to Battle Karts.

'Naira! Angelo!' Gus's voice yells from

somewhere on the other side of Olympus Mons. And I'm so happy to hear it.

We run around the volcano to see all three of them, their faces smeared with sweat-soaked dust, their clothes torn and filthy, but otherwise looking unhurt, running towards us.

I hug Colette tight, even though it notches the pain in my body up at least another level.

'Where'd you come down?' I ask.

'Wait, are you bleeding?' Colette says, pulling back to assess the damage.

'We fell,' Naira says. 'Took a tumble down the volcano.'

'You look like a couple of bad-ass outlaws,' Gus says, seeming way more excited than is appropriate in this situation. 'I should have come with you guys instead of taking the boring route.'

'We went back the way we came for a bit.' Hallie smooths some loose curls off her face. 'Then we crawled fast in random directions – no idea where we were going – but we found a tile that opened up over the bar by Uccellino's. We dropped down on to the roof of it and put the tile back in case Mrs Latchitt went looking . . .'

'It was easy to climb down the sides of the bar,' Colette says. 'We were lucky.'

'One person's lucky is another person's boring as death,' Gus mutters.

'It was weird though, because we could see the whole of the food area from the roof,' Hallie says. 'And it had been totally cleaned out. Like nothing edible left anywhere.'

'Eaten by the Latchitt monsters, I guess,' I say, thinking back to that eye I saw in the lift. The ripped metal. And the scratching, chattering, shrieking noises. Some kind of primate, maybe? I picture overly aggressive spider monkeys with dagger teeth.

'This is why we need weapons,' Hallie says.

'We barely managed to stop Hal from making a bunch of Molotov cocktails from the bottles of alcohol,' Gus says.

'Shoulda let me,' Hallie says. 'We're not

gonna find anything better in this place.'

'But we'll set the Perch on fire and we're locked in.' Naira looks at her like she's mad.

'And no way are we gonna be the people that burned down the sickest place in Finches Heath,' Gus says.

'You're with me, right, Angelo?' Hallie looks at me.

'A fire would activate the alarms and the fire brigade would come,' I say, because although Hal's idea is extreme, it does sound quite fun.

'They've been deactivated,' Colette says. 'We checked.'

'You do realise we could have just pulled the fire alarm if we wanted the fire brigade to come?' Naira says. 'We wouldn't have to start a fire.'

Hallie rolls her eyes.

'Well at least we have a last-resort plan,' I say, patting Hal on the shoulder. 'If all else fails, we explode stuff.'

'So what happened to you two?' Colette asks.

'We got Mrs Latchitted,' I say, glancing at the moon-shaped fingernail holes in my arms.

'She got Angelo and wasn't going to let him go,' Naira says. 'So he . . .' She pauses and shudders. 'He bit her and then we dived through the ceiling and rolled down Olympus Mons.'

'You guys are my heroes,' Gus says. 'That is some GOAT behaviour right there.'

'Oh god,' Colette says. 'You bit her!' The horror on her face matches how I feel when I think about it.

I try not to vomit.

'What did she taste of?' Gus says.

'Gustav!' Naira elbows him in the ribs. 'I'm sure Angelo doesn't want to talk about it.'

'Yeah, maybe too soon,' I say.

'I know we're on a countdown,' Colette says. Forty-three minutes remaining. 'But we should maybe head in the direction of the toilets so we can clean your cuts.'

'Or at least put some wet toilet paper on

them.' Gus starts jogging back towards Uccellino's. 'Plus I need to pee.'

'There won't be cameras in there either,' I say, forcing my stinging legs into movement. 'We can talk.'

We pass the food carts as we run to the toilets – waffles, noodles, falafel – all with bare counters. Every scrap of food gone. The only evidence of it I can see are the gleaming-white bones of what once must have been ribs and chicken wings; their shiny surfaces covered in teeth marks.

'So the Latchitt creatures have, like, locusted all the food in the Perch. Except for the bones,' Colette says.

'Oh great, we're using nouns as verbs again,' Naira says. 'Why does it always come to this?'

'What you thinking, Attenborough?' Gus says.

We're almost at the toilets now, and I can see the table where we were sitting earlier, with the amazing food and the nice Uccellino's server who gave us free desserts. And even though things are bad, I'm glad we at least got to eat before the Latchitts kicked off. And that if we die today we had an A-star last meal.

'I'm thinking scavengers,' I say. 'They ate everything they could find, even the stuff off the floor. Plus . . .' I hesitate, because even as I'm thinking it, I know it's not gonna be good news for us.

'Spit it out, predicter of doom,' Hallie says. 'We can take it.'

'Plus they're smart, and – what's the word? – dexterous. They can get into things. Closed cupboards. High shelves. Small spaces.'

'Sealed lifts,' Naira says.

'So where are they?' Hallie asks, looking around the abandoned Neon Perch.

Gus pushes open the door to the toilets and holds it for me to walk through. 'I'm sure we'll find out soon.'

CHAPTER FIFTEEN

A PEE AND A PLAN

'I know we're here to tend wounds and chat plans, but I'm also actually peeing,' Gus says, scooting past us into a cubicle in the ladies' toilets. We follow, and I lean against a sink before realising I need to pee too. So as much as I would rather not shut myself in another cuboid-shaped cage, I push open the door to the cubicle next door.

'Why are these so much nicer than the

men's?' I say. 'It smells of flowers and the seat's dry.'

'You have a really low bar.' Naira sighs, and I can hear her scouting around, checking for cameras. 'I think we're OK. No cameras or devices other than the smoke alarms, which look legit.'

'So what's the plan?' Colette says. 'How are we going to get a step ahead of the Latchitts?'

'No way will they let us out of here,' Gus says from his stall. 'Sparkly bonus present, my butt.'

'So we need to find our own way out while pretending to play along with their game,' I say.

'And we need to get a message to Mr C at the school so he can evacuate or whatever,' Hallie says.

'But how?' Colette says. 'Our phone signals have been blocked.'

'Well . . .' Hallie says.

'OMG,' Gus squeaks from his cubicle. 'I think Halster has an idea!'

'You don't have to sound so surprised,' Hallie says. 'It's really insulting.'

'Soz, Hal,' Gus says. 'What are you thinking?'

'I'm thinking that to block all phone signals in a building this size, that's literally perched on the top of a hill and has excellent cell service, the Latchitts have to be using a jammer.'

'But how do they work?' I say. 'I have no idea what they even look like.' I push the flush in my toilet.

'Well, I do,' Hallie says. And I can hear the smug in her voice. 'There are different types, but to work effectively on this scale, it can't be a handheld device – it has to be bigger than that. The really big ones are mounted on vehicles, like transit vans.'

'How do you know this?' Naira says.

'Conspiracy theories,' me and Col say at the same time.

'Hal loves a conspiracy theory,' Gus says. 'Especially when it involves corrupt government stuff.'

'Of course,' Naira says. 'So what size jammer do you think the Latchitts will be using?'

I'm about to turn and slide back the lock on my cubicle door, but a splashing sound coming from the base of the toilet stops me. I think for a second it might be an auto flush or something, but it sounds more random and frantic.

'I'd say absolute minimum, the size of a large backpack. Big enough to be easy to find.' Hallie is clearly loving knowing something that the rest of us don't.

I bend down to look into the toilet bowl. Not too close, because gross. But the water is rippling and I can't work out why.

'So we find the jammer and deactivate it . . .' Colette says.

'Or destroy it,' Hallie adds. And I know if she gets the chance she will annihilate that jammer with her bare hands.

'Then we can get a message out,' Naira says. 'Warn everyone at school and call the police – not that they'll be much help, but it might be enough to make the Latchitts leave so that we can get out of here.'

'What do you think, Angelo?' Hallie says.

'Just a sec . . .' I angle my head so I can see where the water pipe connects into the toilet, 'cos I'm sure there's something down there. The water is frothed up, either from the flush or the movement of whatever's in the pipe, so it's hard to make anything out. I lean closer and watch the water churning and lapping up the sides of the bowl. And I know – *I know* – that something bad is about to happen.

Then a solid mass, slick and black, slides rapidly out of the pipe and into the bottom of the toilet like it's been jet-propelled. And as the toilet water splashes violently out of the bowl, all over the walls and floor of the cubicle, and all over me, I swear my heart stops beating for a moment. Because the thing in the toilet is wriggling and scrabbling. The thing in the toilet is alive.

CHAPTER SIXTEEN

TOILET TROUBLE

I jump back and yell out.

'Angelo?' Hallie says.

'What's happening?' I can hear the panic in Colette's voice and I don't want to make it worse, so I try to keep my own voice calm.

'I'm fine,' I say. 'But Gus, if you're sitting on the toilet you'll be wanting to get your butt off that seat, like, right now.'

'Oh god, why?' Gus says. And I hear the creak

of the plastic seat as he stands up.

'What's happening?' Naira says.

Gus lets out a classic Gus scream and I know he's seeing the same thing that I am.

The creature in my toilet sort of decompresses itself, like it had reshaped its entire skeletal structure to be small enough to fit through the pipe. As it stretches out to reveal its true size, swelling bigger, and bigger, my horror growing by the second, it feels impossible that it managed to get through a space that narrow.

Its pointed snout pushes above what remains of the water, a whiskered nose jerking left and right like it's assessing the area, but whether it's looking for danger, or food, or something else entirely, I'm not sure. Then it twitches in my direction, and it's like an alarm goes off in its brain – the snout stiffening and pointing at me like a locked-on missile. The rest of the head fully emerges from the frothy water so I can see it clearly, and it confirms my suspicions about what Latchitt creation we're up against.

'Will one of you tell us what's going on?' Colette bangs on my cubicle door.

I can't tear my eyes away as it emerges, even though I know I should be running. I want a good look at it. Maybe I can spot some mutations – something that might help us to fight it. It's covered in dark fur, slicked flat against its body and greasy from the toilet water. The only non-furry parts are the scaly pink of its clawed feet and curved ears, which are upright and alert – swivelling almost 360 degrees, like scanning radars. It has eyes like marbles – glassy black, but with a red sheen just below the surface that makes them look like they have fires burning inside. It uses needle claws and the powerful muscles in its legs to pull itself up the slope of the toilet bowl, as I back towards the cubicle door. And when it's resting its front feet on the toilet seat while the back end of it is still inside the toilet, I can see that it's going to be about the size of a small cat. Its ears, eyes and nose are still and focused now. On me. Then it stretches the edges of its mouth back, so that the skin is pulled tight against its cheeks, and its four front teeth – two top and two bottom – are fully extended. They must be about five centimetres long. Gleaming yellow and ending in dagger-tip points that are dripping green fluid. It lets out a horrific noise. Like a high-pitched hissing scream. And lunges towards me.

I dodge it, my hand fumbling for the lock on the cubicle door, which I pull back so hard that the sharp end of it cuts into my palm. I burst into the sink area and slam the door backwards knowing it's not gonna make a difference because the creature will easily be able to fit through the gap underneath, but enjoying the thud that it makes as it hits the other side of the door.

Gus is a step ahead of me, covering the ground between his cubicle and where Naira, Hallie and Collette are waiting, pale-faced and wide-eyed, and not quite sure what's happening.

'It's rats,' I say. 'Big ones.'

'Let's go.' Naira starts towards the exit door, but the rat from Gus's cubicle skids out on to the tiles in front of her and scrabbles to a stop, sniffing in our direction, its teeth bared. She screams and pulls back. From the look on her face I'd say that rats are somewhere close to insects in her ranking of creatures she absolutely hates. 'Can they jump?'

I don't want to answer because it's not going to help and we need to get past it and away from these toilets, which apparently are open access for rodent attackers. Gus's rat is around the same size as mine. Darkest brown with fiery eyes. Its tail is at least as long as its body and it coils and uncoils, and flicks and whips, like it has a brain of its own. It reminds me of our battle on the *Melusine*, with a giant octopus who could fully control each one of her arms so that they were even more lethal than her mouth. I'm thinking that this rat's tail is the same: a weapon.

'It tickled my bum,' Gus is saying, like he's having a panic attack. 'That rat tickled my bum with its whiskers. I thought I was having a phantom poo or something. I have that sometimes since I got my stoma – it's like my butt misses pooing so it daydreams about it. And I thought it was a cute poo daydream, but it was *that*.' He points at the rat which is blocking our path.

'It's OK, Gus.' Colette rubs his arm. 'It's OK.'

He's freaking out and we need to get him out of here. Hell, we all need to get out of here, because even though things are bad, I reckon they're going to get a lot worse very fast. Then my rat scuttles out of the cubicle, quickly followed by another, slightly smaller, with patchy grey fur and a tail longer than my forearm. The three of them squeak and hiss among themselves, like they're chatting about the best way to attack us.

'Let me kick them.' Hallie steps forward. 'They look like perfect kicking size.' But I pull her back.

'Look, they all have some weird green substance dripping from their teeth,' I say, pointing. 'And it doesn't look like your standard rat spit.'

'You mean poison?' Naira takes another step back.

'I don't know,' I say, looking around for another way out. 'But maybe. We can't get bitten. It could mean . . . you know.'

Colette and Hallie both swear. We back up some more.

Then the squeaking and hissing stops. The rats fix their focus on us and, with no warning and at the exact same moment, they all leap forward. Demonic eyes glowing. Claws splayed. Screeching so loud it almost hurts my ears.

We all jump back on instinct – that animal need to survive kicking in while our brains are still struggling to catch up – and the rats land on the tiles where we were standing a moment before. They roll and slide on the slippery floor, but it won't be long until they're ready to attack again.

'Stuff this,' Naira says, and she climbs up on to the counter where the sinks are. It's quite high off the ground so I don't think the rats will be able to jump on to it. They'll probably be able to find another way up, but it might buy us some time. I open my mouth to tell the others to get up there too, but they're way ahead of me and already pulling themselves on to the marbled surface. I follow them up, my mind buzzing, trying to think of the best way out of this room.

My nose fills with the smell of synthetic flowers mixed with whatever stench we all picked up in Project Z. The rats are launching themselves towards us but not getting the height they need to make it to the sinks. But it feels like something is missing.

'No nursery rhyme,' Naira says, like she's

been thinking the same thing.

'It literally touched my butt,' Gus keeps repeating, while Colette hugs him and tries to calm him down. To be fair, if I had been sitting on my toilet when the rat came out, rather than standing over it, I'd probably be in shock too.

'No rhyme,' I nod. 'Which means either it could be something we can use to help us control them, or there's worse to come.'

'I say we scram now and worry about that later,' Hallie says.

'Yeah,' I say, looking around again for anything I've missed that might get us out of this rat-infested toilet nightmare. There's nothing we can use as weapons to fend them off. Nothing to lure them away so we can clear a path to the doorway. 'We're going to have to jump and run.'

'Hold up,' Gus says, pulling one of the soap dispensers from the wall. 'We'll squirt, then jump, then run. Aim for the eyes.'

'On it!' Colette grabs another bottle and I take the third one. Then we shower the rats in pink soap slime until they're hissing and screaming and slipping around on their paws. Then we jump, and we run.

CHAPTER SEVENTEEN

THIRTY-EIGHT MINUTES TO GO . . .

We power out of the toilets and back on to the main floor of the Neon Perch, our trainers squeaking against the tiles. It takes less than a minute for the rats to follow, running and skidding after us, and screeching in a way that makes them seem almost supernatural.

We race through the food court, dodging tables and chairs. And while I'm glancing around for the Latchitts' hidden box, it's hard to focus on anything except getting away from the rats.

We make it to Galactic Golf, and I know we can't keep running forever. We need to find somewhere to regroup, or we need to stand and fight.

'Got me a stick!' Gus whoops, picking up an abandoned golf club, and it's actually a perfect rat-battling weapon, so I grab one too, and the others do the same. Around us the golf course has come alive – probably activated by us running across the obstacles – and the quiet of the empty Neon Perch is broken by the electronic victory noises of rocket blast-offs and happy tunes. I wonder which of their senses the rats use to track their prey. From the way they behaved in the toilets, I reckon they're led by their noses more than their hearing.

'Stuff this,' Hallie says, skidding to a stop by

the Solar System hole – the longest hole on the course which involves knocking the ball through each planet at a load of weird angles. 'There are three of them and five of us. We have weapons now. Let's deal with this situation so we can look for the box and get out of here.' She turns to face the oncoming rats.

'Makes sense,' Gus says. He's balancing on one of the rings of Saturn, and he wobbles slightly as he turns. 'I have the high ground so there's no way they can defeat me.'

'Gus,' Colette says. 'There's something happening with the planet behind you.'

'Oh man,' he says. 'I'm assuming it's nothing good.'

The next planet along is smaller, and has multiple holes so that you don't know which one to aim for, more often than not sending your ball spinning out in the wrong direction with a whooshing sound that gets really annoying after the tenth time. But there are no balls rolling through it at the moment, and the whooshing sound is playing on a loop. Something is emerging from one of the holes, black-bean nose first, whiskers quivering.

'Don't say it, Gustav,' Naira says.

It takes me a moment to catch on, and I use that moment to swing my club at the rats who have appeared around the base of Olympus Mons.

'THERE'S A RAT COMING OUT OF URANUS!' Gus yells, and he jumps off Saturn and on to the green, raising his club like a baseball bat.

'Not as exciting, but there's one coming out of Neptune too.' Hallie moves towards it with her club.

The rat's nose jerks in her direction and it pulls itself further out of the hole, red eyes glowing like burning coals. Hallie doesn't hesitate, swinging her golf club back, taking aim before the rat can make a move, and smashing it across the head. It's knocked sideways, rolling off the planet and across the star-covered green, screeching in fury. But considering how hard Hallie hit it . . .

'Minimal damage,' Gus says. 'This guy still has, like, ninety-nine per cent HP.'

And he's right. The rat is already back on its feet and running towards Hallie, like getting smashed in the head with a golf club has really annoyed it.

'And he wants revenge,' Colette says, just as the whooshing of Uranus finally ends and the other rat squats back on its haunches like it's preparing to attack.

The five of us automatically back towards each other into a huddle.

'Five versus five,' Hallie says. 'We can still do this.'

'Six.' Colette points with her golf club at a lighter-coloured one pulling itself out of an astronaut suit.

'We can take them,' Hallie says. 'Six will be a piece of cake.'

'Make that seven,' Naira says. A huge brown monster of a rat has just emerged from the opening of Olympus Mons and is running like lava down the side. 'And we still don't know what they're capable of. Seven is risky.'

'Well, I'm fighting,' Hallie says. And if she's fighting then we all are.

Uranus rat launches itself towards me with a powerful jump that gets it level with the bottom of my ribcage. Its front paws are splayed, curved claws ready to either sink into my skin or slice my throat out, I'm not sure which. Its mouth is open, teeth dripping green. And I'm trying to get a better look at them in the half a second I have before batting it away with my golf club. It thwacks into the volcano, slides down the slope, gives itself a shake and then moves in for another attack.

'We should move,' I say. 'The substance on their teeth definitely isn't normal saliva. They might even have it on their claws too, so a bite or a scratch could mean . . .'

'RIP, Club Loser,' Gus says, swinging his club at another rat who's creeping closer. Just like in the toilets, they're all moving together, and seem to be communicating in high-pitched squeaks. 'You think it's the actual zombie virus?'

'Let's not find out,' Naira says.

'But if we can kill them, we finish the game,' Hallie says, stepping forward again with her club. And I get what she's saying, but it's way too risky.

'Hal, look out!' Colette screams as something furry and black drops from a hanging satellite straight towards Hal's head. Colette rushes forward and pushes her out of the way, and things move so fast that I can barely take in what's happening. Hallie falls forward. The rat thuds on to Colette's back, scrabbling to get a grip on her while she thrashes around to shake it off. But its front claws grip on to her hoodie and it swings there for a moment before rearing back its head and plunging its teeth into her shoulder.

CHAPTER EIGHTEEN

TUNE OF DOOM

Colette screams. The rest of us rush to pull the rat away from her, thinking it will fight to hang on, but it lets go and plops to the ground, backing up a few metres and turning to watch her.

And now the nursery rhyme plays through the Neon Perch's speaker system, booming from everywhere around us.

'*Hickory dickory dock, the mouse ran up the clock . . .*'

'Oh no, Colette.' Hallie is pulling at Colette's

jumper trying to see the wound. 'This was all my fault. I'm so sorry.'

'It's OK,' Colette says. 'It doesn't feel that bad.'

'What are they doing?' Naira is standing guard between us and the rats, golf club ready to swing. But the rats are just sitting. Watching.

'*The clock struck one, the mouse got stung. Hickory dickory dock . . .*'

'Hold up, that's not the usual words,' I say. 'They've changed it. Why?'

'Got stung . . .' Hallie says. 'Colette got stung.'

And I'm not saying out loud but my brain is screaming 'VENOM'. And I feel just this blind panic that's not letting me think straight.

'Guys,' Gus says. 'There's more than seven.'

From every direction, rats are scurrying towards us. Out of holes and cracks, from the ceiling and the escalators, crawling from rubbish bins and food carts. All roughly the same size, in varying shades of brown and black, and with fiery red eyes focused on us like lasers. Actually, no, not on all of us. On Colette.

'I feel strange,' Colette says. She's turned whiter than pale and is swaying on her feet.

'Can you run?' I say. 'We need to run.'

She nods but her movements are off.

'I can't feel my arm,' she says, looking down at it in surprise.

The rats are filling the space around us. Hundreds of them, covering every surface, slinking and rippling like an angry sea.

'*Hickory dickory dock, the mouse ran up the clock . . .*'

And the voice singing the song isn't Mr or Mrs Latchitt, but it sounds familiar. I don't have time to think about it though, I need to focus on getting Colette somewhere safe.

'Karaoke rooms,' Naira says. 'We shut ourselves in. Buy some time.'

'I'll clear a path,' Hallie says, and I can see she's biting her lip so she doesn't cry. She ploughs into the rats between us and Songbirds, kicking and screaming and smashing at them with her golf club. They move when they're forced to, picking themselves back up when they're knocked away and reforming the horde around us without retaliating or getting any closer.

'Angelo,' Colette says. But it's slow and slurred like she's half asleep. 'Can't move legs.' And she stops walking mid-step, her legs locking in place like they're turning to stone. I drop my golf club and catch her just as she starts to fall. I stop her hitting the floor, but can't lift her up properly. She's like a dead weight. And I can't even speak to ask the others for help. I can't do anything except scream internally, long and loud, feeling it sear through my body. Because Colette is staring at me, terrified, a tear rolling down her cheek. And she can't move her eyes, or her mouth to speak, so all that's left is the stricken expression on her face. And I've never felt so helpless.

'*The clock struck two, he stuck like glue. Hickory dickory dock.*'

'Angelo, move now, freak out later.' Naira scoops up Colette's legs and helps me carry her through the lava pool of rats. Hallie in front, creating a path. Gus behind, protecting the rear.

'*Tick tock . . .*'

We're just metres away from Songbirds, and I feel a rush of panic to get there before the song ends. I have a sick feeling that something awful is going to happen when the *Tick tocks* stop. I charge forward, carrying Colette as carefully as I can and elbow the glass door open.

'*Tick tock . . .*'

Nai and I manoeuvre Colette through the doorway and into the karaoke waiting area beyond. If we shut ourselves in, we might not be able to get out. But what else can we do?

Gus and Hallie are behind us, closing the door just as the final *Tick tock* plays out. As the tune ends the rats crush forward like a storm wave, and all I can see is a wall of squirming, screeching rodents. Mouths open wide, razor teeth fully extended, clamouring for the kill. The colossal force of them against the door pushes it inwards, but Hallie and Gus push back, straining to close it.

Nai and I place Colette carefully on one of the sofas and drag the other one to the door, slamming it against the glass and holding the door shut. On the other side, the rats are screaming and frothing, hella mad that they can't get to their prey. They keep flinging themselves at the door, piling against it until it's like a living wall from floor to ceiling, at least three rats deep. The sound of their claws and teeth scraping against the glass fighting a battle against their terrible screeching.

'I don't know if the sofa will hold,' Naira says. 'I'm going to get something heavier. Come help me, Gus,' and she disappears into one of the karaoke rooms, Gus following behind.

Hallie and I brace ourselves against the sofa, keeping it in place while the door judders behind it. She's crying now. Looking anywhere in the room but at Colette.

'It's not your fault,' I manage to say, though the words come out in a kind of gravelly growl because my mouth is painfully dry.

Hallie just keeps crying so I squeeze her hand. Wanting so desperately to go to Colette so she doesn't feel like we've abandoned her, but knowing I can't move away from the door until it's properly secure. And scared to go to her in case . . . I can't even let myself think it.

The karaoke room door thuds back against the wall and Naira backs out carrying one end of a coffee table. Her face is red with the effort and she's struggling to keep moving, so it must be heavy.

'You'll need to get the sofa out of the way. Move when I say,' she says, without looking up.

'Got it,' I say.

Gus follows, holding the other end and

managing better than Naira – I guess all that weight training is paying off. They get it in position next to the sofa and Nai rests her end on the floor for a second, bracing herself for a final push.

Me and Hallie raise up into crouches, still holding the sofa in place until the others are ready.

'Go!' Naira yells, and we slide the sofa to the side at the same time as she and Gus heave the table in front of the door. We all step back for a second, the rats still piling against the glass. The table holds, the door doesn't budge.

I run to Colette who hasn't moved even a fraction from where we left her, lying face up on the sofa at the other end of the waiting room.

'I'm here, Col,' I say, kneeling next to her and more terrified than I've ever been when I see how pale and still she is.

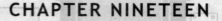

CHAPTER NINETEEN

WAKE UP

I feel like I can't breathe. 'Angelo.' Naira holds my arm gently. 'Let me check her.'

And I don't want to let go of Col's hand, but Naira is calm and smart and I trust her. So I move aside, sobbing like I haven't since I was Raph's age.

'Get a mini disco ball from one of the rooms,' Naira says, her fingers on Colette's neck.

Gus runs back through the door to where they found the table and brings a football-sized disco ball back to Naira. There's a moment as

192

he passes it across that I can see my horrified face reflected in a thousand tiny squares of mirror and I can hardly recognise myself. Naira holds the ball close to Colette's nose and mouth and peers at the glass.

'She's breathing,' she says, finally.

'You sure?' I say.

'Look.' Naira points at the surface of the ball nearest to Colette's mouth. Every few seconds it clouds, like shower steam on the bathroom mirror.

'Thank god,' Hallie says.

'She has a pulse too,' Naira says. And she takes my fingers and puts them on Colette's neck. 'It's faint, but steady.'

And I'm too messed up to be able to feel anything. So I take a deep breath. Force myself to quiet. Close my eyes. Focus every bit of calming energy on the nerve endings in my fingertips touching Colette's neck. And I feel it. The gentle flutter of her pulse as her heart pumps blood around her body.

'We should try to place her on her side,' Naira says. 'Everyone lift her gently on three.'

We each put our hands under Colette, gently and carefully.

'One, two, three . . . ' Naira says, and we roll her over so that she's lying on her left side, facing across the waiting room. Her arms and legs are still rigid, like they've been frozen in place, and I think about how in animes when characters are frozen with ice powers, sometimes their bodies shatter into millions of pieces. We arrange cushions around her, trying to keep her safe, or limit the damage, or whatever we can. The problem is that we have no idea what we're dealing with.

In a burst of frustration and anger, I punch the wall below the Songbird Karaoke sign. I feel the skin over my knuckles split and blood spill, but I don't care. I pull back my fist for a second blow.

'Angelo.' Hallie grabs me and holds me back. She's shaking, and I'm shaking. And I know punching a wall isn't going to help any of us, so I stop fighting and slump to the ground. Hallie bear-hugs me so tight it hurts a little bit, but it's what I need.

'If Colette can hear us, she needs you, Angelo,' Naira says. 'Let's sit with her while we try to figure out what to do.'

So we sit on the floor in a semicircle, facing Colette on the sofa. I'm by her face, holding her hand, which feels all kinds of strange because it's not holding mine back.

'Could really do with a hot choccie right now,' Gus says. 'Where's Mr C when you need him?'

'They'll still be at school, right?' I say. 'If Mr Hume is talking it'll go on for hours.'

'Very true.' Gus nods. 'And here I was selfishly thinking that we were the ones having the worst day. We should pray for those poor souls in the school hall.'

And I can't laugh right now. Maybe I'll never be able to laugh again. But I appreciate his effort to get us back on track and I feel myself relax, just a little. And in that moment I feel something else – the slightest movement in Colette's hand.

I bounce on to my knees and look into her face, scared that I imagined it but sure I didn't.

'She moved,' I say. 'I swear to god, she moved.'

And Nai, Gus and Hal are next to me, staring at Colette, willing her to do it again.

For maybe five seconds there's nothing. But then her eyelids move, just a flicker.

'You see that?' I say, my entire body surging with adrenaline and hope.

'I saw it,' Naira says. She feels for Colette's pulse again. 'It's getting stronger.'

'Come on, Colette,' Hallie says. 'Whatever's happening to you right now, just fight it with everything you have.'

'Otherwise we'll carry you into one of the karaoke rooms and give Naira the mic,' Gus says.

She moves again, way more visible this time – a mini jolt of her body, like she's trying to snort out a laugh in that way she does when Gus says something funny in a serious situation.

'What are we thinking?' Naira says, repeatedly taking Colette's pulse, like a doctor wired on energy drinks.

Colette's fingers put pressure on mine. She blinks.

'Some kind of temporary paralysis?' I say. 'Maybe? Please let it be that. Please?'

'Seems like you're putting a call into the universe for some vibes,' Gus says, and I'm not looking at his face 'cos I'm staring at Col, but I can practically hear him raise his eyebrow.

'Don't believe in vibes,' I say. Although I swear I'd believe in anything if there's a chance it could make Colette better right now.

Her mouth twitches, like she's trying to talk.

'Lucky for you, the vibes transcend your disbelief,' Hallie says. 'Thank you, vibes.'

Colette's chest is visibly rising and falling with

each breath now. Her eyes are moving across our faces. She's getting stronger by the second.

Naira looks at her watch. 'It's been about ten minutes since the bite and the "Hickory Dickory" song.'

'So the toxin takes the length of the song to fully kick in . . .' I say.

'. . . Making the bitten person paralysed while the rats gather,' Naira says.

Colette can move her head slightly now. Her arms and legs too.

'So if that person was alone, they'd be stuck in the middle of the rat swarm with no way of running or fighting,' Hallie says. Now that the worry for Colette is easing off, I can see anger filling the space it's leaving behind. 'The rats would have ten minutes to . . . to . . .'

'Eat,' Gus says. 'Like literally gobble the person up.'

'And they'd be powerless to do anything about it,' Naira says.

And the horror of it stops all of us in our

tracks. We know the Latchitts are capable of doing evil things – of hurting and killing in the pursuit of their goals. But this is next-level stuff. We look at each other, pale faced, shaking, and I don't think anyone breathes for a full ten seconds.

'Guys,' Colette says, pulling us back to the moment, and I look down to see the pinkness returning to her cheeks.

'Thank god,' I say, kneeling in front of her and helping her to sit up.

'Don't thank god, thank vibes,' Hallie says, and she's holding Col's other hand and looking like she might cry again.

'How are you feeling?' Naira asks, checking Colette's pulse again and looking right into her eyeballs like she might find the solution to everything there.

'I feel . . .' Colette pauses, takes a deep breath. 'I feel normal. The bite is hurting, but I'll take that any day over feeling nothing at all.'

'May I look?' Naira asks, and Colette leans forward so Naira can check the wound.

'What did it feel like when the poison started working?' Gus asks, unzipping Kitty and rummaging around.

Colette bites her lip. 'It felt like I was dying.' Her eyes fill with tears but she blinks them away.

'The bite is clean,' Naira says. 'You'll need to get it looked at, but I can't see anything bad around the puncture marks to suggest the toxin is still there.'

'So that's good,' I say, my overwhelming panic lowering down another notch. I look at Colette's face – a face I feel like I know as well as my own – and the ordeal she's been through is written all over it.

'I don't have hot choccie, but I do have this.' Gus produces a wrapped, cube-shaped sweet and puts it in Colette's hand.

Colette gasps. 'Is this what I think it is?'

Gus nods slowly. 'It's the last-ever piece of

Melusine artisan fudge. I've been saving it for a special occasion. Was thinking about giving it to you for your birthday so I brought it with me. Then I got to thinking that we all get birthdays every single year, like, they're way too meh for the world's most special confectionary . . .'

'Yeah, you're always so meh about your birthday.' Naira side-eyes him. 'What was it this year? A whole weekend of Gus-themed events including a bouncy castle with your face on it?'

'And all the Gus food,' Hallie says. 'Apple crumble and GUStard, GUSty bread rolls . . .'

'Confusingly also hot dogs and GUStard,' Colette says.

'Don't forget all the stuff that included asparaGUS,' I say. 'That was a real highlight.'

'And yet I didn't eat the final piece of *Melusine* fudge,' Gus says. 'So I rest my case.'

'Your birthday is in June. We hadn't even been on the *Melusine* then,' Naira says.

'I don't see how that's relevant,' Gus says.

Naira rolls her eyes and stops arguing.

'My point is that I was saving it for a once-in-a-lifetime, peak-exclusivity event. And that time is now.' He nods at Colette. 'It's what the *Melusine* would have wanted.'

'But I can't,' Colette says. 'It's too much.'

'You really should,' Naira says. 'Your body has been through some serious shiz in the past fifteen minutes and the sugar will help with the shock.'

'OMG, Naira said shiz,' Gus gasps. 'A sign, if ever there was one, that things have got drastic. Eat it, Colette. Eat it.'

'Well, now I feel like there's too much pressure,' Colette says, and she's trying not to laugh, which is the most brilliant thing to see.

'Would you like us to turn away and give you a private moment with the fudge?' I say, and I'm smiling, and Hal and Gus and Nai are smiling.

'I feel like Gus needs the private moment.'

Colette smiles back. 'To say goodbye.'

'I just want to remind everyone that we still have a situation to deal with,' Naira says. 'So if you don't eat it in the next thirty seconds, Colette, I'm going to throw it out to the rats.'

Gus gasps. 'Don't you dare!'

'Eating it right now,' Colette says, and she starts unwrapping it. 'And because I don't want Gus's sacrifice to be in vain, let's work out how the hell we're getting out of here.'

CHAPTER TWENTY

NAIRA'S DARK SECRET

'I don't know about you guys, but I feel like listening to some really loud music,' I say, trying not to laugh at Gus watching Colette eat the fudge like she's eating his firstborn child. I don't say it, because we still don't know if the Latchitts can hear us, but it would be good to have some noise cover while we talk.

'Good idea,' Naira says. 'I'll put some on.' She jumps up and pushes open the door to one of the karaoke rooms, propping it open with a chair. 'Any requests?'

'Why do I feel like you've been here before?' Hallie asks. 'You seem very familiar with this place.'

'Erm . . .' Naira says. Her back is to us and she's using the touchscreen to activate the karaoke system. 'That's not important right now.'

'You come here by yourself, don't you?' Gus's face lights up. 'You come and you sing your heart out. Like a secret karaoke addict!'

'You never do!' Hallie gasps.

Naira keeps pressing and doesn't say anything.

'OMG, you do!' Colette says. 'You actually do!'

'You have to tell us, Nai,' I say. 'Because this may be the only good thing to come out of our being hunted by human-eating rats situation.'

'They have half-price sessions on weekday mornings in half-terms and holidays,' Naira sighs. 'And you get points towards free sessions every time you come. So it's only a few pounds for an hour. And I really want to get a part in the school production this year, so . . .'

'So you come here to practise?' Colette says. 'That's adorable.'

'So adorable.' I nod.

And Naira comes out of the room, her cheeks burning red, as a backing track starts blasting out of the speakers.

'Ooh, I love this one,' Gus grins.

'I know,' Naira says. 'A reward for your sacrifice. Now let's stop talking about karaoke and make a plan. Angelo, what are you thinking?'

I resist the urge to ask her what she sings when she comes here and store it in my mind for a later time. 'So the way I see it, we have two options. We're safe enough here unless the rats chew through the walls. If that happens, we could retreat into one of the karaoke rooms – aka Naira's secret hangout – to buy more time. We could stay. Refuse to play.

The meeting at school won't last forever and at some point Mr C is going to come back for us.' I don't want to say it but I'm worried to move Colette. She seems OK, but like Naira says, her body has just been through something massive, and having to run or fight might be too much for her.

'But the live stream,' Colette says through a mouthful of fudge. 'If we don't play, they'll attack our families at the school.'

'Will they, though?' Naira says. 'Remember that Mr Hume is in that hall, and we're ninety-nine per cent certain he's a Latchitt ally. If they send rats into the school, he'll be in as much danger as anyone else.'

'Unless he knows how to control the rats like the Latchitts do,' Gus says, smoothing out the fudge wrapper in his hand and tucking it lovingly back into Kitty. 'Because they've been moving around the Perch, right? And they haven't been eaten, so they must have a way of staying safe.'

'How are they staying safe?' I say. ''Cos they're not singing, or at least Mrs Latchitt wasn't when she was in the roof. So they must have another way.'

'What do we know about the rats?' Naira is retying her ponytail, which feels strangely reassuring in this bat-poop crazy situation.

'Do you want me to braid your hair, Colette?' Hallie asks. She hasn't left Col's side since she woke up, I think because she still feels like it was her fault. 'I could do, like, a halo braid and keep it all out of the way so you're ready for action.'

'Yes please.' Colette smiles. 'That would be great.'

'Do you want me to put yours in a man bun, Angelo?' Gus says. 'You know, seeing as we're apparently getting our hair battle-ready.'

'Here, I have a spare band.' Naira pulls a pink elastic off her wrist and hands it to Gus who sits behind me and starts smoothing back my hair.

'Guess I don't have a choice,' I say. 'But we should also get back to the rats.'

'Sure, sure,' Gus says. 'What are you thinking?'

I close my eyes for a second and try to calm my pulsing brain so that I can focus. And as Gus's hands and arms waft close to my face, I get a noseful of the rank smell we got sprayed with in Project Z – the smoke, the fake blood, the water. And it hits me.

'We know their dominant sense is smell,' I say. 'They're obviously drawn towards whatever filth we have all over us, thanks to the Latchitts. So it's likely that the Latchitts are using scent to repel them too.'

'You're done,' Gus says, moving around me so he can see my hair from every angle. 'And looking hot, if I may say so. Like a less genocidal Eren Yaeger.'

'Er, thanks,' I say.

'Shame we can't do something with mine,' Gus says. 'I feel a bit left out.'

'There are some cowboy hats in the prop boxes in the karaoke rooms,' Naira says. 'You love a hat.'

Gus gasps and scampers through the open door into the karaoke room. 'I'll put on another song while I'm here,' he shouts.

'There's a really pretty pastel pink one that I wear sometimes,' Naira says, all dreamy like she's looking back on a summer romance or something. Then she suddenly snaps out of it. 'So what scents repel rats?'

'I think garlic,' I say. 'But I didn't smell that on Mrs Latchitt, and she was breathing right into my face.' I shudder at the thought. 'But you know when I bit her and Gus asked me what she tasted like? I swear she tasted minty, which I wasn't expecting.'

'She def doesn't give off mint vibes.' Gus comes back out of the room wearing a navy blue cowboy hat that's covered with little diamonds. 'Just call me the midnight cowboy,' he says in a Texan accent. 'And I would have thought that there lil' ol' lady would taste like dusty saddles an' desert grit.'

The next backing track starts playing.

'Ooh, Taylor Swift!' Colette squeaks. 'Thanks, Gus.'

'That's my pleasure, ma'am,' Gus says, winking and tipping his hat at her.

'And in Project Z,' I say, 'they kept blasting us with that smoke that smelled fresh and herby. And we know there were rats in there with us a bunch of times but they didn't attack. Then after we got soaked in the meat-rot stench, they properly came after us. It's the smell. Their attack mode is triggered by smell.' And I shudder again 'cos the Latchitts have been in control since we set foot in the Neon Perch. They could have murdered us at any time. 'They went to a lot of trouble to set up this game,' I say.

'All those months in prison cells,' Hallie says. 'They must have been hella bored.'

'So we know mint is good – yay for mint,'

Colette says. 'But unless Gus has a tube of toothpaste in Kitty, I don't know how we can use this information to help us.'

'No toothpaste,' Gus says. 'No fudge either now, sadly.'

'Mint or no mint, our main issue is that even though the Latchitts could be bluffing about attacking the meeting,' Hallie says. 'We can't risk it, can we? We have to play the game so they don't go through with whatever they're threatening, or we have to eliminate the risk by eliminating them. You know what my vote is for.'

'OK, so we actually have three options,' I say. 'Stay here, play the game, or try to take out the Latchitts.' I stand up and walk to the spot in the wall that I punched a few minutes ago. There's a fist-sized hole in the first layer of it, which is only a plasterboard-type material, so not surprising that I broke it. But behind there are multiple layers of waxy foam fabric, about four centimetres thick.

'This stuff must be for the soundproofing,' I say, trying to feel through it to find out what's behind. 'Whatever the exterior wall is built from, it's solid.' I rap on it with the non-bleeding knuckles on my right hand. 'I don't think the rats can chew through it, but equally I don't think we can get out this way either.'

'And the ceiling?' Colette says. 'Could we go up?'

Naira climbs on to the counter in the back corner of the room and knocks on the ceiling. There aren't tiles in here like there are everywhere else. 'I think it's made from the same stuff as the walls,' she says.

Gus disappears behind the counter and starts opening whatever drawers and cupboards are there.

'You're getting way too comfortable with petty theft.' Naira raises an eyebrow as she climbs down to see what he's doing.

'Thug life.' He grins.

'So we're safe but we're stuck,' Colette gets

up and walks to the glass door where the rat rampage seems to have calmed down. It's like they've realised they can't get in and they don't want to waste their energy. But they're hanging around outside in case we come out – I guess we're their best chance of a juicy dinner now that they've cleared out the rest of the Perch. Rats are smart. 'How do we get out?'

'The "Hickory Dickory" song,' Hallie says. 'Which, by the way, is the stupidest name for a song ever. When the tune was playing the rats pulled back. Just 'cos the Latchitts aren't using it doesn't mean it won't work for us. Could we try?'

'We could,' I say. 'But I think there's a reason why it was a recording and not just the Latchitts whistling or singing it.'

'Found a can of Coke,' Gus says, lifting it up and opening it without a moment's hesitation. 'And yeah, what was with that laid-down track? Like they paid someone to record it for them.' He takes a swig of Coke and sighs happily. 'So good.' He passes it to Naira.

'Did you guys not think the person singing sounded just like Colette?' I say. 'I wonder if they used technology to reproduce your voice?'

'Sounds like the sort of creepy-ass thing the Latchitts would do,' Hallie says.

'They should have got someone better.' Colette sighs. '"Hickory Dickory" (Taylor's Version) (Ten-Minute Version) for the win.'

'I kind of liked how they changed up the lyrics to make them fit the monster, though,' Gus says. 'Gotta respect the grind.'

Naira passes the can to Colette and runs into the karaoke room. 'We can test this really easily. I'll grab a mic.' She comes out with an old-school microphone and flicks up a switch on the side to turn it on. 'I turned the volume up to maximum, so with the door open the rats should be able to hear it.' She holds out the mic. 'Who wants to try?'

'It should definitely be you, Nai-Nai,' Gus says.

'For sure,' Colette says as Hallie passes the Coke to me and I gulp down a mouthful. It's like the nicest Coke ever. 'You've been practising.'

'You won't laugh?' Naira says. And Naira hardly ever gets shy so it's quite sweet.

'Do it, Nai,' Hallie says.

And Naira does it. She sings 'Hickory Dickory Dock' like she's belting out a power ballad in the finale of a West End show. And you know, it's not that bad. Better than before anyway.

We watch the rats.

Their ears swivel towards us when the tune starts and there's a second or two where I think it might be working. But then they start barging into the door again.

'Maybe it was my horrible voice,' Naira says.

'Na-ah, no way,' Gus says. 'You sounded good. Solid seven out of ten.'

'Thanks,' she says. 'But Col should try it too, because she sounds more like the recording.'

So Col takes the mic and gives it a go, but

with the same result as Naira's effort.

'If singing the song doesn't work,' Naira says, switching off the mic, 'how are we going to get out of here?'

'I know a way,' Hallie says, standing up like she's just made a momentous decision. 'We can use the song but it has to be the Latchitt version.'

'But that's only going to play if someone gets bitten,' I say. 'There must be some kind of sensor that activates it – a microchip inside the rats, maybe? It would make sense that the Latchitts have put implants in them so they can keep track of their movements – they're valuable assets, I guess, and we know the Latchitts have access to some bad-ass tech.'

'You mean like the chips they put in dogs in case they get run over?' Gus says. 'Then the vet knows who to pass the bad RIP news on to?'

'Well, that's hella dark, but yeah,' I say. 'A more advanced version of those that can measure blood levels and stuff – sense when the rat has made a bite and released the toxin. It would mean the Latchitts have more control.'

'So then the tune won't come on, unless . . .' Colette says. Then she pauses. Looks at Hallie in horror. And it takes me a second or two to catch on to what she's thinking.

'That's right. Someone has to take one for the team, get themselves bit so that everyone else can carry on.' Hallie has a steel in her eyes as she looks around at us all. 'That someone is going to be me, and there's nothing any of you can do to stop me.'

CHAPTER TWENTY-ONE

TWENTY-ONE MINUTES TO GO

'Absolutely no way,' Colette says. 'That is not happening.'

'It's happening,' Hallie says, and she's already walking to the door. 'Like I said, I'm doing it and you can't stop me.'

'Hal, wait.' I run and stand between her and the coffee table that's the only thing between her and rat-bite horror. 'We need to think this through.'

She stops in front of me, hands on hips. 'We

don't have time. The clock is ticking, and a load of people are at risk. So move, or I'll kick you in the balls.'

Naira comes to stand beside me. The karaoke backing track has auto-skipped on to some old rock song which I think is called 'The Final Countdown'. Funny.

'Hal, we can spare a few minutes to make a proper plan,' Naira says. 'So just stop for a second.'

'Please, Hal,' Colette says. She stands on the other side of me, no sign of the paralysis that made her so helpless a few minutes ago. That rat toxin is incredible, and, not for the first time, I think about how insanely smart the Latchitts are and how much good they could do if they channelled it in a more wholesome direction.

'You know, it's not the worst idea for one of us to get bitten and use the time to get out of here,' I say. Because of course I don't want Hallie to sacrifice herself – I'd rather be the one to do that. But I know her and I know there's no point arguing. 'If Hal really wants to do it, we should let her.'

'Plot twist!' Gus gasps.

'But we make it work for us,' I say. 'Get her somewhere safe until the toxin wears off and use it to end this nightmare of a game.' I look at Hallie. 'So?'

'I'm listening,' she sighs.

Naira points at the hole I made in the wall. 'We could use the insulation in the walls to protect us, tie it around us like armour.' And she's already pulling away the plaster so she can get hold of the foam panels. 'If we control as many of the variables as possible, we can take away a lot of the risk.'

Hallie nods. 'Sounds like a plan I'm willing to go along with.'

'So we use whatever we can to protect ourselves so the rest of us don't get bitten and can carry Halster away,' Gus says. 'I'll get the prop boxes.'

'We can wrap this stuff around our forearms and lower legs.' Naira is pulling thick foam sheets out of the wall. 'So we can fight better and defend ourselves. But where are we heading when we get out of Songbirds? Just running aimlessly is not going to end well.'

'You're right,' I say. 'We'll just end up in another trash-fire situation. Or we'll keep running and fighting until we're out of energy and easy pickings.'

'We need to find the phone jammer so we can warn Mr C,' Hallie says. 'It's going to be somewhere central in the building to make sure its range extends far enough.'

'The security office,' I say. 'It's right in the middle of the ground floor – the centre of the Perch in all directions.'

'How do you know that?' Hallie asks.

'A few years ago I tried to steal a bunch of five pences from the coin pushers,' I say. 'If you shove them in a certain spot, you can tip them enough to slide a whole stack of coins

down the chute. I wanted some curly fries . . .'
I shrug and stop talking. Embarrassed about
the stealing. Ashamed that we never had
enough to eat no matter how hard my parents
worked, even though I know it wasn't our fault.
'Security guards shut me in the office and
called my mum.'

'This is excellent,' Naira says. 'Except that
the security office is exactly where the
Latchitts are going to be so they can watch us
on the cameras.'

'Which actually makes it the safest place in
the Perch as far as the rats go,' I say. 'They're
not going to go near if the Latchitts are there
with their minty repellent properties.'

'They won't be expecting us to go there
either,' Colette says. 'I bet they haven't even
locked the door.'

'This is a plan.' Hallie grins. 'We can go to
the security office, destroy the jammer and
fight the Latchitts. All my dreams come true.'

'Except you'll be a living statue,' Colette

says. 'You won't be able to smash anything.'

'Oh yeah.' Hallie's grin drops off her face instantly. 'Oh man, that sucks.'

'I'll take the bite so you can fight,' Colette says.

'No.' Hallie shakes her head. 'I'm doing it. And maybe missing the fight is the true sacrifice. Although I'd really appreciate you guys stringing it out for as long as possible so I can at least get a bit of action.'

'We've never taken the fight to them before.' I run to the wall and help Naira pull out the lengths of soundproofing material. 'We spend all our time running from them. Even when we lured them to the Bookery, it was to trap them with the vamps, not to fight them ourselves.'

'They're hella strong.' Gus pulls another box into the room and starts rummaging through feather scarves and giant plastic sunglasses. 'But there are two of them and five of us, or four until Hallie unfreezes. That's still good numbers.'

224

'And all we need to do is keep them busy while one of us deals with the jammer,' I say. 'Distract them for long enough to get a message out.'

'We should preload the messages on our phones, so we just have to press send as soon as the jammer's out of action.' Colette is kneeling on the floor, pulling inflatable guitars out of the prop boxes.

'I'm hoping this means that you're down with the plan,' I say. We're building a huge stack of useful stuff and it's like my hope is growing along with it.

'I want it to be done,' Colette says. 'I'm so ready to fight.'

Gus whoops. 'Then let's suit up and kick wrinkly evil old people butt.'

And we work as fast as we can to make the best of a bad situation, which too often in life is the only thing you can do. We shield each other from the cameras as we tap the same message into our phones:

DANGER: DWH being watched with threat of Latchitt creatures. CL trapped in NP with Latchitts and toxic human-eating rats xx.

We spend most of our prep time arguing about how many kisses to put on the end. We wrap ourselves in white spongy armour, tied on with rainbow bunting and Sellotape. We stuff inflatable musical instruments up our hoodies to give an extra layer of protection. We grab what we can to use as weapons – the golf clubs, some tambourines, a pack of spearmint chewing gum we find in one of the drawers – literally anything that won't weigh us down too much and might be useful.

'Tell me I'm not rocking this look,' Gus says as we stand, braced, by the coffee table, ready to slide it away from the door and plunge into the rat ocean outside. 'I feel like every time we're in a life or death situation we should create a new clothing line inspired by it.'

'Apocalypse chic,' Hallie says. 'We totally have it nailed.'

'Look at you, little mice, in your raggedy finery.' Mrs Latchitt's voice suddenly squeaks through the speakers. 'I must say that I admire your determination, sweetlings, even if it is misplaced. Our beautiful ratty rats will bite through your efforts in minutes – it won't keep you safe.'

'Ah, she's ruined it now,' Gus huffs.

'She always ruins everything,' Colette says.

'Eighteen minutes left,' Mr Latchitt says. 'And then we finish this.'

'We're finishing it sooner than that,' I say, making sure my face is turned away from the camera. And I realise that as scared as I am, I'm also impatient – excited almost – to get on with whatever's coming next. 'Everyone ready?'

'So ready,' Colette says.

'Yep,' Naira says. 'You good to go, Hallie?'

Hallie nods.

'I'm the midnight cowboy,' Gus says. 'I was born ready.'

'Then let's do this,' I say, and I grip the edge of the coffee table, ready to slide it away from the door. 'One, two, three . . .'

The table is out of the way in one swift movement. The glass door is open. And we charge back into the Perch, padded up like hockey goalies, gripping our golf clubs and ready for whatever comes next.

CHAPTER TWENTY-TWO

LUCKY THIRTEEN

We have a clear plan and know exactly what we're doing, but we don't want the Latchitts to know that. So we act chaotic, which is really, really easy for us. We make sure that everything we do and say, we do with added drama. Wide eyes. Hand gestures. That sort of thing. And we have thirteen minutes left on the clock.

I look around the first floor of the Perch like

I have no idea where to go next. The area around Songbirds is rat saturated. They're sitting around in groups, chattering among themselves like gossiping mums on the school pick-up.

'I guess their training didn't prepare them for a siege in a karaoke room,' I say.

'It's like they're discussing what to do.' Naira turns three-sixty, checking out the space beyond Songbirds.

'Or maybe they're just chatting about peng tings and opps,' Gus says.

We take a step forward and the rats in the closest group stop squeaking and sniff the air.

'Peng tings and opps?' Naira says. 'Really, Gustav?'

'You're super smart, Nai-Nai, but do you speak rat?' Gus says. 'I don't think so.'

Eight pointed snouts face in our direction, red eyes flaring.

'I don't speak rat either,' I say. 'But I'm pretty sure that, like me, they're thinking about dinner.' And I take another step, then break into a jog.

There's a ripple of murky fur and coiling tails as more and more rats notice us. I try to estimate how many there are as I lead the others towards the centre of the first floor. There must be at least three hundred here. From the look of them, all adult rats – strong and healthy.

'Imagine if they get loose in Finches Heath,' I say.

'Rats breed fast, right?' Colette asks.

'Yeah,' I say. 'Crazy fast.'

Then a big black rat – I swear the same one that came out of the toilet at me earlier – looks me right in the eye, then raises itself up on its back paws and screeches.

'This dude's holding a grudge,' I say, maintaining eye contact because as creepy as his hellfire eyes are, you don't let anyone beat you in a stare-out.

And the rats attack.

They surge forward, grouping and regrouping

so that I can't see where they start and end. If I manage to force a gap in their ranks with my golf club, it refills almost instantly.

'You think if they have rat babies, the kids'll inherit the toxin genes?' Colette shouts, using her forearm to fend off a pair of charcoal greys who leap towards her face. Their claws hit the waxy foam armour and can't get a grip, so they plop down like dirty fat raindrops and are absorbed into the rat puddle at our feet.

'I'm gonna guess yes,' Hallie says. 'Ma and Pa Latchitt will have made sure of it.' She kicks a rat hard in the head and it falls back, just to be replaced by another three.

'Four!' Gus yells, and he gets a powerful shot off against a gnarly-looking rat with oversized paws, sending it flying into the Galactic Golf counter.

But there are too many of them, and we've stopped making progress. We're huddled. Trapped about two metres from the escalators.

The rats are crawling over my feet and trying

to climb my legs, scratching and biting. The padding is keeping me safe, for now, but they'll soon find some skin to sink their teeth into.

'We can't go any further,' Naira says.

And that's the code word.

I let one of the rats pull itself higher up my body while I pretend to be busy knocking away a chunky one that's come from above and landed on Gus's cowboy hat. Hallie is ready. As the rat on my thigh opens its mouth with a shriek, its oozing teeth bared and stabbing towards my leg, Hallie reaches out to bat it away. Its teeth sink into her hand. She shouts out in rage and rips it off, throwing it back into the swarm.

The music starts to play.

The rats that are latched on to us let go and drop to the ground, rejoining the pack. Reforming the army.

'Hallie,' Colette screams, and her distress seems genuine. I know we planned for this, but it's still awful, seeing the pain and fear in

Hallie's eyes. Of course she'll say she's faking, but having witnessed what happened to Colette when she got bitten, there's no way she's not scared.

'*Hickory dickory dock, the mouse ran up the clock . . .*'

'Get on, quick,' Gus says, crouching down in front of Hallie. She climbs on to his back, arms around his neck, legs around his waist. Gus is the strongest of us, so it makes sense for him to carry her. And I'm thinking that maybe I should be working out too, 'cos who knows when one of your friends is going to be bitten by a toxic rat and needs a piggyback, mid-battle.

'*The clock struck one, the mouse got stung . . .*'

'Let's move,' Naira says, and she looks around like she's trying to work out which way to go, even though we all know where we're going.

'How you doing, Hal?' I say, as we kick our

way through any rats standing in our path and finally reach the escalators. Naira first, then Gus with his Hallie-shaped backpack, then me and Colette.

'I'm OK. I just feel weak, like my body is falling asleep,' Hallie shouts back.

'*Hickory dickory dock . . .*'

Instead of stepping on the escalator, Naira vaults herself on to the central section – a shiny silver metal surface that slopes down beside the steps.

'I've actually always wanted to do this,' she says, and she pushes herself off, sliding down fast to the floor below.

'*Hickory dickory dock, the mouse ran up the clock . . .*'

Gus gets on next, with a bit of difficulty 'cos he's carrying a whole extra person on his back. But he and Hal are whooshing down in a few seconds, with Naira waiting to catch them at the other end. Then Colette's up and sliding, and I'm right behind her, just as the rats start to follow us, knocking into each other in their rush to jump on to the slide.

'Which way now?' Colette says, as we tumble off the bottom.

'Getting stiff,' Hallie says, her words distorted like when someone talks through chattering teeth when they're cold.

'We need to find somewhere safe for Hallie,' I say. I point at the Battle Karts arena, where there's a maintenance shed with spare wheels and stuff for the go-karts. It's beyond the security office so the Latchitts will think we're carrying on past them. And I'm getting hella nervous, because if that office door is locked and we can't break it down, we're going to be rat food.

'The clock struck two, he stuck like glue . . .'

'Let's do it.' Naira starts to run. The path ahead is clear of rats, I think because all of them are behind us and catching up quickly, so we can move as fast as it's possible for Gus to run with Hallie now fixed on to his back.

'Not being funny,' he yells. 'But I must look awesome right now. I feel like a Teenage Mutant Ninja Turtle, but with a bad-ass hat instead of a mask.'

'*Hickory dickory dock . . .*'

'Those masks are so pointless,' Naira says. We're about twenty metres from security. 'Like, they do nothing to disguise them. You can still clearly see that they're Ninja Turtles.'

'But they look cool, Naira,' Gus says. He's breathing heavily now. 'You've got to respect the aesthetic.'

'And they help us to tell them apart,' Colette says. 'I don't mean to be rude, but the turtles all look basically the same.'

'*Tick tock . . .*'

'Colette, that is so offensive to the Ninja Turtle community,' I say. Ten metres from the door. 'They're really easy to tell apart.'

'*Tick tock . . .*'

And that second *Tick tock* is the sign. We change direction, turning right and barrelling towards the security room door – turtle Gus with a now rigid Hallie clinging to his back, then Naira, Col and me. We don't hesitate and we move as fast as we can, closing down the last few metres until we literally crash through the door and straight into whatever situation we're going to find behind it.

'*Tick tock.*'

CHAPTER TWENTY-THREE

DOUBLE TAKE

Colette was right: the door isn't locked. I guess the Latchitts' arrogance is one of the few things we can use against them. We charge into the security office like a SWAT team storming a terrorist hideout – hard and loud. We know that the element of surprise is going to be our strongest asset. Well, that and our absolute fury about everything the Latchitts have done to us, our families and our friends.

Because of my previous brush with the Perch

security guards, I know the security office is separated into two parts. The main room when you enter has a bench for troubled teens to sit on while they wait to be collected by angry parents – an uncomfortable, creaky strip of wood on metal legs that's perfect for making someone think about what they did. Time passes differently when you're sitting on that bench, butt cheeks aching, and dreading the inevitable telling-off, grounding and/or loss of phone and games console that's looming in your near future. The air smells the same as the last time I was here, like sweat mixed with fast-food lunches. The bin is overflowing with balled-up napkins and food packaging, and I'm briefly distracted by wondering if the security guards get free tacos.

On the right, behind the desk, is a partition wall, with a door that leads to the business end of security – the smaller room that contains all the secret stuff. It has a bank of monitors on one wall where you can watch all the Perch action from the CCTV. We'd assumed that this is where the Latchitts would be sitting, enjoying their evening viewing of us fighting for our lives. Again, we were right.

As we burst into the main room, Mr Latchitt is just raging out of the partition door, his face twisted in fury. His stint in prison hasn't decreased his size or strength from the look of it – if anything he's even bigger than he was the last time I saw him. His dark shirt is tight over his shoulders and back, his biceps visible through the fabric. The only big change is in his face where he wears a black patch over his right eye. The rumours about him losing it to the vampire birds must have been true. It doesn't seem to be holding him back though, and it enhances the look of seething anger that's radiating out of him. I've never in my life seen someone so physically intimidating. But this is not the moment to get scared.

Naira and Gus step out to the sides, leaving me clear to run straight at him. I swing back my golf club and drive it hard at his knees, making him fall forward but not completely topple. Naira and Gus dodge past him and into the second room. He lurches forward on his knees and swipes at Colette as she tries to get behind him. She screams. Crashes into the wall and bounces back towards him, the force of it making her unable to stop herself. He grabs her wrist in one of his giant bear hands, and jerks her towards him. I try not to panic as she cries out in pain and attempts to pull away from him, then cries out again as the movement hurts so bad she turns white. I don't know how she's going to get out of this. So I swing back the club again, ready to take advantage of any opening and take him down properly this time.

'You brats,' Mr Latchitt roars, tightening his grip on Colette's arm and dragging her towards him, so close that his spit is flying in her face. 'How dare you attack us? We make the rules.' Beyond him I hear the sounds of a fight, and Mrs Latchitt screaming. I remind myself that

Gus, Hal and Naira can handle it and try to block it out. Behind me I hear the screeching of hungry rats in attack mode, but I don't have a second to turn around and see if they've followed us into the room. My full focus needs to be on Mr Latchitt, and on getting Col away from him. Colette is struggling against him, but he's recovering from the shock and the blow to his knees, and starting to get to his feet again. If he does that, we'll never be able to knock him down and the whole plan will fail. So I look for a chance, bracing myself to take a swing at him as soon as there's an opportunity. But of course he's holding Colette between us like a human shield.

'You will never beat us,' Mr Latchitt bellows in Col's face. 'You're weak. Pathetic.'

Colette stops struggling suddenly and stares him right in the eye, which is just about level with hers.

'Col, duck,' I yell. Ideally I want to get him in the knees again but I don't see how it's possible with Colette held in front of them. She can't get away but she might be able to crouch. And honestly I don't want to hit anyone around the head with a golf club, even Mr Latchitt – the thought of it makes me feel sick. But I'll do it if I have to.

'No,' Colette says. 'I've got this.' And I'm shocked, and scared to back off, but I can see from her face that she is so done with this shiz. So I respect it, and take a step back. Col needs to fight her own battle with Mr Latchitt. I have half a second to wonder how she's gonna play this – he's at least five times thicker than her and twice the height. But he's still on his knees so their heights are equal for now . . . She aims a swift, brutal kick at his groin and he gasps in pain, letting go of her arm. He tips forward, his hands clutching his crotch, his eyes glazed with tears. Hell, my eyes are watering and I'm not the one who took the kick to the balls.

'Come on.' Colette pulls me forward and through the door into the partition. We close it and lock it, leaving Mr Latchitt rolling around on the floor behind us.

'I'm going to feed you to the rats,' he yells, but it's nicely muffled by the locked door between us, which also acts as a spit barrier. 'And if you lay a finger on them, I'll finish you all.'

'Them?' I say, because surely he means 'her'. He's worried about us doing something nasty to Mrs Latchitt, obviously, with him out there unable to protect her. I'm about to turn around to see if Naira and Gus (and statue Hallie) have managed their part of the plan, but Mr Latchitt is already up and thumping on the door. It's shaking in its frame with each blow and I know we don't have long. I glance around for something to help barricade it, like the sofa and the coffee table in Songbirds, but the scene my eyes fall on is so mind-blowing that for a moment I freeze up like I've been rat bitten.

Mrs Latchitt is sitting in a wheeled office

chair, pinned in by a golf club that's been slid through the loops of the armrests and then wedged into the corner of the room. The ends of the golf club are pushed tightly into the angle where two of the walls meet, and Naira is holding it there with her foot. Mrs Latchitt is screeching and cursing in a way that doesn't sound human, and her hair is wild like she's just run through a hurricane. She thrashes around in the chair, trying to free herself, making the sides of it scrape against the walls as it turns and jolts. But for now she's stuck. So that should be it. Mr Latchitt is locked out. Mrs Latchitt is trapped. They won't stay that way for long but all we need is a minute to smash up the unguarded phone jammer.

Except the phone jammer isn't unguarded. There's someone standing at the other end of the room, holding it. Like Hallie said, it's about the size of a backpack, and it has about nine or ten antennas poking up out of the top. But no one's looking at the jammer.

I open my mouth to speak. Close it again. I look across at Naira who has one eye on Mrs Latchitt and one eye on the person holding the jammer. Her eyes flick to mine, just for a second, and then to Colette. She shakes her head slightly like she has no clue how to deal with this situation.

Gus and Hallie are standing a few metres from the third and completely unexpected member of Team Latchitt, just staring. I mean, Hal has to stare 'cos she can't move her eyes due to paralysis, but I swear I can see the same horror in them that I see in Gus's.

'What do I do?' Gus says, jiggling up and down, looking from the phone jammer, to the person holding it, to Colette.

Colette is corpse white. Just staring.

Mr Latchitt is throwing himself into the door like a human battering ram.

Mrs Latchitt starts laughing like a rabid hyena.

The person holding the phone jammer is

about the same age as us, maybe a little younger. Similar height and size, just maybe a little smaller. She's cradling the heavy-looking equipment like a teddy bear, and looking at us with such hatred that I wouldn't be completely surprised if we all burst into flames and died from the ferocity of it. Her honey-coloured hair frames a pale, heart-shaped face, dotted with the final remains of summer freckles. It's a face I've looked at more than almost anyone's – a face I know like my own front door, like the pattern of my bedroom wallpaper, like the view of Raph's top bunk over my head as I'm lying in bed. A face that's been one of the best parts of my world for what feels like years. And I can't get my head around it. It's like my brain is rejecting what my eyes are seeing. Because the face of our new enemy, standing in front of us, protecting the thing we need to destroy, is Colette's.

CHAPTER TWENTY-FOUR

TIME STANDS STILL

'Who the hell are you and why do you have my face?' Colette says to the girl we don't know. The girl glares at Colette but says nothing.

'It was you in the lift,' I say. It wasn't Colette . . . it was this *fake* Colette.

Colette spins around and takes a step towards Mrs Latchitt who's cackling in her chair in the corner. 'Who is she?'

'Isn't it obvious?' Mrs Latchitt says. 'She's a

better version of you, little bird.'

'But she's . . .' Colette says, looking from the girl to Mrs Latchitt and back again.

'She's our granddaughter,' Mrs Latchitt hisses like a cornered cat. 'And thanks to you troublesome little mice, she's all we have left.'

I can't stop staring at the girl. Scanning her face for any differences between her and Col. Her face is more rounded, maybe. And she doesn't have the scar by her eye that Col got in the vamp attacks.

'I know,' Gus says. 'Col had an identical twin that you snatched from the hospital just after she was born, then you somehow adjusted everyone's memories to forget she existed.'

Mrs Latchitt laughs again.

'How would they adjust the memories of Ms Huxley and a whole hospital full of staff?' Naira says.

'I've seen it done before. Many times,' Gus says. Hallie is still sitting on his back, totally still, and we can't even check if she's OK.

'We've discussed this before, Gustav. Movies don't count.' Naira pushes harder on the golf club keeping Mrs Latchitt stuck in the chair. 'Even ones that have Zendaya in them.'

'And she's younger,' I say. 'She looks more like start of Year 7 Colette.'

The girl turns her angry eyes on me, and the look she gives me is something so close to the look Col gave me when I stole from her back when we first met that I have to look away.

'Or dressed-by-your-grandparents Colette,' Gus says, staring at the girl's outfit: smart skinny trousers with leather boots, plain tucked-in T-shirt, all in boring colours. 'No offence, I mean you're wearing it well, it's just a bit work-placement Barbie meets horse-riding Barbie.'

'Yeah, you look like you're going for an interview for head girl at a posh school,' Colette says. She's mad. And confused, which is making her more mad.

I'm trying to put the pieces together while

not making eye contact with not-Colette who is making me horribly uncomfortable. Mrs Latchitt is looking at her with, like, pure joy . . . and pride. Pride. Like this girl's existence is because of her. And I know what the Latchitts have done.

'You . . . created her,' I say to Mrs Latchitt. 'From Colette's DNA.'

'Always the clever one, wily fox,' Mrs Latchitt says. 'But not as clever as us, sweetling. No, we have achieved something no one else in the world has.'

I notice that Mr Latchitt has stopped thumping at the door. He's listening.

'Holy freaking scrutbags,' Naira says. 'You actually went there. You made a human clone.'

'What did you expect, sweetlings?' Mrs Latchitt says. 'We had a precious new granddaughter in the hospital who we knew we might never get to treasure. So we slunk in. Took what we needed. Then grew one for ourselves. Our precious . . .'

'Wait, I know!' Gus says. 'Clonette!'

'It's Corinne actually,' the girl snarls at Gus. 'And I am nothing like her – the only thing we have in common is our DNA.'

'That's quite a lot, though,' Gus says. 'Just saying.'

Colette and Corinne stare at each other and I can't even begin to imagine what's going through their heads. This is a LOT.

'If we really do have the same DNA,' Colette says. 'Then you should know better than to stay with the Latchitts. They're evil.'

'You're evil,' Corinne says. 'You killed my father.'

'We've been through this already,' Colette says. 'We didn't kill him. I'm sorry you lost him but it was his fault, not ours.'

'That's not what I heard,' Corinne says. I mean, if she thinks we killed her dad, no wonder she's salty. She's grown up with the Latchitts so she's probably got a messed-up view of the world.

'We've always kept our hummingbird tucked away, nice and safe,' Mrs Latchitt coos in a creepy baby voice. 'But she insisted on being here this time, to watch you all suffer.'

Mr Latchitt starts on the door again, and I remember that we don't have long to do what we came here for. But I feel like I can't tackle Corinne – it would be all kinds of wrong.

'Can we have the jammer?' I say to her, nodding at the device in her arms.

'Obviously not, idiot,' she says. 'Your hands are unpleasantly sweaty, by the way. I hope I never have to touch you again.'

'Whoa,' I say, holding my hands up. 'No need for the insults.'

If she's not going to give it to us then we'll have to take it. We just need her to let her guard down for a second so we can go for the jammer without attacking her. Because we can't attack her. She might be a Latchitt, but it's not her fault.

'You know you're on the wrong side here,

right?' Naira says. 'You might not see it now, but we can explain everything to you. You don't need to be Team Latchitt.'

'Totally room for one more member of Club Loser,' Gus says. Which is actually surprising because he always says we can't let anyone else in. 'I can make up another badge.'

Colette takes a small step closer to Corinne.

'Hold on,' I say. '*I* don't even have a badge.'

'You're too moody and edgy for badges,' Gus says. 'It would ruin your look.'

'Do you have one?' I ask Naira.

'Of course,' she says. 'It's on the inside of my school blazer.'

'That's where we wear them, to make it secret and cool,' Gus says. 'Don't we, Hal?' He pats her leg, and I swear I can see it move a little like she wants to kick him. It would be a really good time for the rat toxin to wear off because we clearly need her help.

I turn to Gus. 'But if we have to wear them on the inside of our blazers, how would it ruin my look? Nobody would see it.'

I can see Corinne in my peripheral vision, looking at us like we're the weirdest people she's ever been unlucky enough to meet. Colette is poised. Ready.

'Listen, Angelo,' Gus says. 'You give off no-badge vibes. I assumed you wouldn't want one and I'm sorry. If I'm making one for Corinne anyway, I can easily make one for you. How about it, Corinne?'

She puts all her focus on Gus, eyes fixed, mouth open like she's about to call him the worst possible name she can think of.

And then Colette moves. She lunges at Corinne, flinging herself at her legs. It's a good shout – just like with Mr Latchitt, a surprise unbalancing is probably her best chance. And with Corinne holding the jammer, she's top heavy and can't put her arms out to steady herself. They both crash to the ground. Mrs Latchitt shrieks. Mr Latchitt roars. Gus and I both dart forward, hoping to help in some way in what might be the most awkward scuffle ever, between my girlfriend and her evil clone.

Colette and Corinne are in a tangled pile, two pairs of arms wrapped around the jammer, both rolling and scrabbling and trying desperately to get the upper hand. Col is slightly taller and probably fitter and stronger, but she's exhausted from everything we've been through at the Perch. Maybe still feeling the effects of the rat toxin. And the homemade armour she's wearing seems to be getting in her way as much as it's helping to protect her from some of Corinne's blows. I can't call it.

'Help, for god's sake,' Naira yells at us. She can't move from the corner without freeing Mrs Latchitt. 'Get the jammer.'

So Gus and I stand over them, trying to reach in and wrench the device away, but we can't get a grip on it. The girls are fighting so viciously that we both get kicked and headbutted multiple times. And I worry that I'm making things worse for Colette instead of better.

Then I hear a voice I haven't heard for about ten minutes. And it's brilliant to hear it for a few reasons, one of them being that we have our best fighter back in action.

'Drop me,' Hallie says. She's stiff and slow but trying to detach herself from Gus, so he throws both himself and her down to the ground next to Col and Corinne, and Hallie sort of rolls off him.

'Hair!' she yells. And from somewhere deep in the battle, Colette hears her. She lets go of the jammer and grabs Corinne's hair, which is loose and easy to grab. She yanks Corinne's head back, pinning her down while Hallie clambers on top of them both like an enraged sloth and flicks a switch on the phone jammer.

'Should have done your hair in a halo braid,' Colette yells, letting go of Corinne at the same time as a bunch of beeps from our phones tells us they're back in action.

'Word is out,' I say to Mrs Latchitt who has fallen still and silent in her chair. Seething with hatred for us. Thinking. Plotting. 'Everyone at Dread Wood High knows what's happening and help will be coming. What's your next move?'

And then there's a thundering crack as the wooden door splits from its hinges and Mr Latchitt explodes into the room.

CHAPTER TWENTY-FIVE

THE LAST STAND

He shoves Naira, hard. She flies across the room, smashing into the desk below the banks of CCTV screens and crumples to the ground. Gus is there in a second, helping her to sit up. I turn back to see that Mrs Latchitt has freed herself and she and Mr Latchitt have regrouped by the open door.

'Come along, hummingbird,' she says to Corinne, who is picking herself off the floor.

'It's time to fly.'

And it feels wrong to let this girl, who looks so much like Colette, go to the two most hideous people I have ever known and be a part of their remorseless violence. I step in front of her.

'Don't go,' I say, aware that Colette is looking at me like I've lost my mind. 'Stay with us. We can help you.'

'I don't need your help, you filthy reprobate,' Corinne hisses at me.

'Let her go, Angelo,' Colette says. 'She's a snake. She's totally twisted and we could never trust her.'

But I stand my ground, just for another second or two, finally having the courage to meet her eyes. I stare at her. She stares back. I'm looking for the smallest chink in her anger – a speck of doubt about the Latchitts. But her eyes are hard and cold and full of disgust. So I watch her go to her grandparents, remembering that our aim was never to stop them from getting away, it was only to make sure they couldn't hurt our families.

I feel the comforting vibration of my phone as it rings in my pocket. That urgent buzz that says someone needs me. Or that someone wants to know I'm OK. And I reach for it, planning to answer. To hear my dad's voice, Raph in the background chattering away whether anyone's listening to him or not. But of course the Latchitts have other plans. They aren't finished with us yet.

'Oh, sweetlings, you have got yourselves in a pickle,' Mrs Latchitt says, She's holding tightly to Corinne's hand and they're already heading out of the door. 'Our ratties will devour you long before help arrives. All they will find is your bones.'

'There's no escaping them this time.' Mr Latchitt smiles. And it's such a rare thing that I can't tear my eyes from his face – neat white teeth, too small for his mouth, glinting in the artificial light.

'Dude really wants us to die,' Gus says, his arm around Naira, helping to steady her while she gets the strength back in her legs. Colette and Hallie are standing together – a fierce unit with no intention of being rat sacrifices.

I'm scared – of course I am – but I'm sure the security room door will hold long enough for us to think of a plan. The second the Latchitts are gone, we're barricading ourselves in.

Then the Latchitts run. Mrs Latchitt and Corinne at the front, with Mr Latchitt following. They're through the main security room and at the doorway with no fear of the rats who I can see dotted around in groups like they were when we escaped from Songbirds. They sniff the air as Mrs Latchitt and Corinne move towards them, and scatter away. Mr Latchitt pauses a moment, giving us one last grin as he points at the hinges of the main door. And it's like my heart implodes because as my eyes focus in on the small metal parts that hold the door securely in the frame, I can see that he's

messed with them. The screws are half out.
The rectangular plates lopsided.

'No!' I rush towards him, but I'm too late.

He aims a powerful kick at just the right spot
on the door to finish it. The screws ping out and
the hinges fly off in a shower of splinters. Then
he throws what looks like a small glass bottle on
to the floor in the open doorway, gives us one
last flash of that nasty grin, and he runs.

The door is trashed. The liquid from the
bottle is puddling on the tiles between us and
the rat army, and it stinks. Same as the smoke
in Project Z. The rats are already twitching
their noses towards it.

'What do we do?' Hallie says, looking around
for some kind of inspiration. 'It's not going to
take long for the rats to start attacking again.'

'Can we go up?' Gus asks, running to the desk
in the second room and climbing up. It's too
low to get to the ceiling from, so he tries
putting his weight on one of the monitors to
see if it will hold.

'Seems solid,' he says, bouncing up and down on it a couple of times. But it buckles suddenly and smashes on to the desk, sending shards of glass and pieces of metal and plastic shooting across the room, and Gus falling on to his butt. 'Or maybe not.'

Five or six rats are investigating the stink juice and taking their first steps into the room.

'I guess that potion is counteracting the mint repellent that the Latchitts were using,' Naira says. She's scanning the room – I expect she's looking for a way out or for something we can use against the rats. Same as I am. But there's no back door. No way up into the ceiling.

'Grab your weapons,' Hallie says. This is gonna get messy.'

We pull ourselves on to the table in the main room, huddled up back to back in classic Club Loser fighting formation, as the rats start scurrying into the room.

'We can last until someone comes to help us,' Gus says like he's trying to reassure himself as much as the rest of us. 'We're a bunch of bad-asses.'

'Let's hold them off for as long as we can,' Naira says. 'If someone gets bitten the rest of us pick them up and force a way out of here. Try to find somewhere we can shut ourselves in.'

'Where's that Pied Piper guy when you need him?' Gus swings at a red-eyed rat that's venturing towards the table.

'Oh yeah, the Pied Piper from that weird kids' story,' Colette says. 'I'd forgotten about him.'

A rat is pulling itself up one of the table legs. Colette kicks it off.

'The who now?' Naira asks.

'The Pied Piper. He's a creepy, pointy guy who visits a town with a rat infestation . . .' Gus says.

'How is he pointy?' Naira asks.

'He wears, like, a pointy hat and those pointy shoes from olden times,' Gus says. 'Anyway, he tells the mayor he can get rid of the rats if they pay him some gold. The mayor agrees

. . .' He stomps on the paw of a rat that's made it up on to the table. The rat screeches, drops down to the ground and immediately starts climbing up again. '. . . But after the Pied guy gets rid of the rats, the mayor does him dirty and refuses to pay. So Pied comes back and steals all the children from the town.'

'That's seriously dark,' Naira says. 'How is it a kids' story?'

I remember it now. Pictures of a sussy-looking man playing a pipe that hypnotises both rats and children. Randomly.

'He uses music to lure them away,' Hallie says.

'Maybe he's the Latchitts' OG inspiration.' A rat grips on to Colette's ankle and she kicks it away.

'Except I think our man Pied is no friend of the rats. He leads them off a cliff or something,' Gus says.

'I thought he drowned them in the river.' Hallie stomps on the tail of an especially big and nasty-looking one.

'Either way, he gets rid of them for good,' Colette says as a rat flies at her. She uses her armoured forearm to bat it away. 'Which would be really useful right now.'

I risk a swift glance at Colette's face. She's still pale – the rosiness in her cheeks hadn't come back properly after the rat-bite situation, and then she had to deal with the shock of finding out she has an actual clone.

I feel sick. I feel tired. And I'm so done with these rats. There are about thirty of them in the room with us – all desperate to take a bite. I imagine them running loose in Finches Heath. No one would ever be safe. We need to contain them. Trap them somewhere they can't escape. Then us and our friends and our families will be OK and I can make things right with Col. And I make a decision, right here, right now. No time to question it. No time to discuss it with the others.

I leap off the table into the swarm of rats.

CHAPTER TWENTY-SIX

DRASTIC ACTION

'Angelo!' Colette yells. 'What the hell are you doing?'

'Pied Pipering them,' I yell back while kicking my way through the rats as fast as I can. I need to get further before I'm bitten.

'Where?' I hear Naira's voice, clear and calm, through the onslaught of rats springing at me from all directions.

'Ice rink,' I shout. I'm out of the security office now and heading back towards the escalators and the skating rink beyond. It's a fair distance – maybe eighty metres – and there are rats everywhere.

I hear a scream from back in the office and my heart lurches, thinking one of them has been bitten, but the tune doesn't play. So I keep moving, covering the ground slower than I'd like. Rats are dropping from the ceiling now – I guess we led the way up there earlier and now they have the run of the crawl space. I shake the first two away, but as I'm ripping one off my T-shirt, its razor claws embedded in the material, I see a dark shape falling towards me. I dodge, but not quick enough. It lands half on, half off the side of my head. Scrabbles to get more purchase. Fails and slips. But as it slides it makes one last attempt to grab on. There's a sharp pain at the top of my left ear that makes me gasp. And I know instantly, even before the music starts playing, that I've been bitten.

'*Hickory dickory dock, the mouse ran up the clock . . .*'

The rats fall away and I run. Happy in the knowledge that Col, Naira, Gus and Hal have some time and space to get away, even if it means leaving me behind. Rats are hurtling towards me from every corner of the Perch. Not attacking, just swarming. Waiting for the toxin to fully kick in so they can attack. I push the thought away. Focus on running.

'*The clock struck one, the mouse got stung, hickory dickory dock . . .*'

I think of Raph sitting in the school hall with his space book, his tufty hair looking like he's just woken up no matter how many times Dad smooths it down. Smelling of milk and cookies. I hope everyone at the meeting is safe now. That our families are out in the winter cold, breathing the chilly air. Mr C pep-talking everyone and helping them to stay positive. I can see the sign for Penguins Ice Rink in front of me. Way ahead, but a target to aim for. I can't feel the left side of my face. Keep running.

'*Hickory dickory dock, the mouse ran up the clock . . .*'

My arms and legs are getting heavy and I still have a way to go. I try to ignore it. Keep driving forward. I think about Club Loser – the best friends I have ever had. The best friends I will *ever* have. Naira being the smartest, most together person I've ever known, keeping calm when the rest of us are freaking out. Gus with his cowboy hat and super strength, sacrificing his fudge and making us laugh no matter how bad things get. Fearless Hallie. They've all changed so much since we were forced together just over a year ago on that cold November Saturday.

'*The clock struck two, he stuck like glue, hickory dickory dock . . .*'

I'm almost out of time. I'm slowing down. I think of Colette. The shock on her face when she saw Corinne. The hurt in her eyes when I tried to stop her from leaving. If I wasn't mostly numb, I swear the memory of it would physically hurt. Eyes forward, Angelo. Penguins is a few metres away now, the doorway to the rink wide open so I can just bowl straight on to the ice. That's good.

'*Tick tock . . .*'

I know the rats are a seething mass behind me and it's kind of lucky that I can't move my neck enough to turn and look at them. It must be a terrifying sight. My body is lead trying to swim through concrete. It's falling into a coma even though my brain is wide awake. Just a bit further.

'*Tick tock . . .*'

I'm on the rink, pushing myself as hard as I can so that the ice can do most of the work for me. I'm limping and skidding, trying to stay on my feet. If I fall, or if I don't get to the other side before I fully freeze up, I'm dead. And I want to tell Colette that the reason I wanted to help Corinne was for her. Because as scared and furious as she is about Corinne right now, when those feelings die down she might realise that she wants to know her. Like a sister or something. Someone with that much of Colette in them – sure without the daisies or hand-drawn tattoos and with a massive attitude problem caused by her Latchitt upbringing, but at her core the same person – can't be truly bad. I'm a metre away from the back barrier of the rink, and I'm slipping. With one last effort, I put my arms out to help me keep my balance. And then, just centimetres away but out of time and no longer able to control my body, I stop.

'*Tick tock.*'

Strange to be unable to move even the tiniest bit, but with almost heightened senses. I can hear everything. Feel everything. So I'm aware of the screeches of the rats. Of the scritch scratch of their claws as they pull themselves up my body. Of the sting as their teeth find the places on my skin that aren't protected by padding. It hurts. And I'm scared.

'We're coming, Angelo.' Colette's voice rings

out through the noise of the horde. 'Hold on!' And I don't want her to be here but I'm so glad that she is. And now I can see her. And Naira. And two pairs of arms reach over the back barrier, grabbing my outstretched ones and hauling me up and over the glass wall. The sting of it scraping the skin off my chest and stomach is probably the best pain I've ever felt. The weight of the rats lessens as some of them fall off, and while Colette holds me steady, face down, half over the barrier, so all I can see is the floor, Naira uses a golf club to hit the rest of them back down on to the ice.

'You're an idiot, Angelo,' Colette says. And even though I can't see her face from this angle, I know that she's crying. 'Don't ever do that again.'

And then I'm being pulled the rest of the way over. I'm out of the rink and away from the rats, and I'm so freaking grateful.

Colette and Naira prop me against a pillar and dart away, but I'm facing away from the ice rink so I can't see what's happening.

'Gus has shut the gate,' Naira shouts – to Col, or to me, or to someone else, I don't know. 'We just have to stop them from climbing out until backup arrives.'

'On it,' Colette yells, and because I can't see what she's doing, I try to picture the scene in my mind. I imagine them running the perimeter of the rink, pushing back any rats that get close to climbing the barriers. They're chest height and made of sheets of thick, smooth plastic that's shaped to look like glaciers. They should be hella hard for the rats to get a grip on, but there might be weak spots where a skating collision has left a dent, or some scratches in the surface. They could really use another pair of hands and I curse myself for being useless.

'Angelo, you crazy son of a gun.' Gus's voice suddenly appears in my ear, making me inwardly jump but outwardly remain statue still. 'That was some big G energy.' I feel his hands gripping me in my armpits, and he turns me around so I can see. He grins in my face and pats me on the shoulder. 'Hal's on her way and you'll want to see this.' Then he runs off, the diamonds on his hat reflecting rainbows on everything around him.

I can only see things directly in my field of vision. Penguins Ice Rink stretches out in front of me – the ice enclosed by plastic glaciers, and cartoon penguins sliding down snowy slopes. The rink is more rat than ice, a bubbling lava pit of furry bodies and fiery eyes. Now that I'm not directly in front of them, the rats seem unsure about where to go. They shriek at each other like they're arguing, nipping at the rats around them with their teeth. There's no hierarchy that I can see, which means there's no leader for them to follow. So instead they run back and forth, looking for an exit.

'I have supplies!' Hallie whoops from the far side of the rink, and she bombs into view, swinging a large backpack off her shoulder and unzipping it in one smooth movement. 'Angelo, hey!' she yells, grinning at me as she pulls large bottles out of the bag, handing one each to Naira, Gus and Col. They unscrew the caps and run the perimeter of the rink, pouring the contents down the inside of the glacier barricade. It's glossy, gloopy liquid that oozes stickily down the plastic and on to the ice.

'Mint syrup.' Gus grins at me, waving his bottle as he coats the area directly in front of my pillar. 'They had some in the coffee bar for the fancy frappes.' Then he turns back to the rink. 'You hear that, rats? Prepare to "mint" your doom.'

It's genius. The syrup makes the walls super slippery, and the rats are disgusted by the smell. They stop trying to climb the glaciers and retreat into the middle of the rink. Colette, Naira and Gus toss their empty bottles on to the ice and run back towards where I'm lamely propped up against the pillar.

'Go for it, Hallie,' Naira yells, and I'm wracking my brain to work out what else they have planned. And then Hallie pops up from behind the barrier on the other side of the rink, grinning like a demon. And I really should have guessed. I mean, it's Hallie.

There's a flare of light that starts at Hallie, then soars through the air, crashing down into the mass of rats.

'She's only flippin' done it,' Gus says, punching the air. 'Hallie, my G!'

As the missile hits the ice, it explodes in a ball of flame, making the rats shriek and hiss. Then another fiery bottle hits, and another, and soon I can't see the rats through the flames and smoke.

Colette comes to stand beside me, tucking herself against my chest so that it's almost like I have my arm around her. And by the time we hear the sirens outside the Perch, I can put my arm around her properly.

CHAPTER TWENTY-SEVEN

FOOD, FRIENDS AND FUTURE THOUGHTS

'This is going to get old really, really fast,' Hallie sighs.

We're sitting in her house, cosy in the den area, which is full of the comfiest sofas and the magical glow of fairy lights.

'I don't know,' Gus says, rolling himself off a fat chair and towards the coffee table that's loaded with food. 'Your parents do a grazing

280

table better than anyone else I've ever known. Luxury artisan foods for days. Like this . . .' He picks up a bite-sized piece of something that looks like pastry with red-flecked green stuff and possibly cheese, and puts it in his mouth. 'I don't even know what it is but it's the GOAT of snacks.'

'But they're never going to let us go anywhere on our own again,' Hallie says. 'Trust me, you'll get bored of the food.'

'Literally never happening,' I grin, piling my plate with a variety of unknown posh-food goodness.

'And it's only until the police catch the Latchitts,' Colette says, taking a tiny cream-coloured cube with a strawberry on top of it off my plate as I snuggle in next to her. I feel a bunch of scabs peel off my hundreds of wounds as I sit, but I don't care. It could have been so much worse.

''Cos they did such a great job of that last time,' Hallie says. 'Because they're already back on the streets and terrorising us.'

'We agree with you, Hallie,' Naira says. Her two broken fingers are strapped together with surgical tape that Gus coloured pink for her. I still feel bad about crushing them in the crawl space so I pass her one of her favourite biscuits from my stack of food. 'Of course we do. But right now there's nothing we can do about it, so we should use our time in parent jail to rest up, recharge and get ready for whatever's next.'

'Now, now.' Mr C comes in carrying a tray of mugs. 'You're not in parent jail, you're in protective custody. Totally different thing.'

'And yet it still feels like an attack on our personal freedom,' Hallie says.

Mr C slides the tray on to the table and sits cross-legged on the rug.

'How's the WhatsApp live session going?' I ask. I can hear the buzz of chat from the kitchen where all of our parents are having another 'meeting with nibbles'. It's painful but it means we get to spend time together, so we just leave them to it.

'So far we've all agreed that it's still unsafe for you lot to be anywhere other than home or school . . .' Mr C says.

'I don't see why school is allowed when we know Mr Hume is part of the Latchitt conspiracy,' Hallie says. 'Surely it's dangerous for us to be there too.'

'We still don't have any proof of that,' Mr Canton says, passing mugs of hot chocolate around to us.

'Come on, Mr C, you know it wasn't a coincidence that he called you all in for an unnecessarily long and boring meeting on the same night that the Latchitts set their trap,' I say. 'He's one hundred per cent Team Latchitt.'

Mr C takes a sip from his mug and does a weird sigh that's like half hot choccie happiness and half we're in a hellish situation sadness. This is our lives now, and has been for over a year. The best of the best and the worst of the worst all together. 'Look,' he says, straightening his back and lifting his chin like he's about to launch into a classic Mr C pep talk.

'Here comes the choccie chat.' Gus grins.

But we're saved by the ring of the doorbell.

Mr C gets up. 'That'll be the police. They said they'd be sending some officers over today.'

After a few minutes of murmured conversation at the front door, the two police officers walk into the den. We've never met these ones before, so I take a good look at them, trying to work out if they can be trusted. Or if they're absolute scrutbags like the last two police who were looking after our case.

'Hi,' one of them says, smiling at us. 'I'm DS Jobling, this is DC Azam.' She nods at the guy next to her.

'It's good to meet you,' Mr C says. 'We were expecting Detectives De Salis and Ajao . . .'

'They've been reassigned,' Jobling says. 'So we'll be working on your case from now on.'

'Can I get you both a drink?' Hallie's mum pokes her head into the den. 'Tea? Coffee?'

Jobling points at the mugs of hot chocolate we're holding. 'Any chance of one of those? They look incredible, right, Azam?'

'Heck, yes.' He smiles. 'I never say no to a hot chocolate.'

Mr C's little face lights up, and we're all biting our lips so we don't laugh because it's really cute.

'Of course,' Hallie's mum says. 'Would you like whipped cream? Marshmallows?'

'Yes please. All the good stuff,' Jobling says, and Hallie's mum disappears off to make their drinks.

'Well, you've already passed the test.' Mr C smiles at them. 'Can I ask why De Salis and Ajao were reassigned?'

Jobling and Azam exchange a look.

'To be honest with you, some questions have been raised over their handling of affairs,' Jobling says.

'In particular the situation with the missing evidence that caused the case against Mr and Mrs Latchitt to collapse, as I believe you were told at the scene of the attack.' Azam perches on the arm of one of the sofas. 'On behalf of Finches Heath police we sincerely apologise. We know there have been failings and that these put you all in grave danger.'

We all just stare at him. I don't think any of us know what to say.

'There will be an investigation,' Jobling says. 'But for now our focus is on catching the Latchitts again, and making sure they stay off the streets for good. That's why we've come to talk to you today – may I sit?' She points at the space on the sofa next to me. I nod.

'So we've been unable to trace them since they left the Neon Perch,' Jobling says. 'The CCTV footage from everywhere in the vicinity of the building was corrupted and unusable.'

'Here are your drinks.' Hallie's mum comes in with hot chocolates, and Jobling and Azam look delighted as they take giant swigs.

'That hits the spot,' Azam says. He has a bit of whipped cream stuck in his beard, and I find myself liking him even though I know we have to be careful – it feels like the Latchitts have half the town in their pockets.

'If you remember anything else about what they did or said, please do give us a call,' Jobling says. 'Even if it seems insignificant. We need to build up a picture so we can anticipate their next move.'

'Of course,' Mr C says. 'We'll let you know if we think of anything.'

'And to keep you fully informed,' Azam says, 'we wanted to let you know that we've also been looking into Corinne. As we expected, there are no records for a Corinne Latchitt or Lachey at all – no birth certificate, school files, medical history – nothing. On paper she doesn't exist. We'll keep digging, of course, but it seems like the Latchitts have done a good job of keeping her hidden from the world.'

The Corinne situation is still awkward – especially for Colette and her mum who I think doesn't know how to feel about it. It's like she has another daughter, I guess. A daughter she's never met who hates her.

'We don't talk about Clonette,' Gus whispers, grimacing and doing the slit across the throat gesture. An uncomfortable silence settles in for a few seconds.

'Try not to worry too much,' Jobling says finally. 'The entire force is looking for the Latchitts, and they'll have to surface at some point. We'll find them.'

I'm not sure any of us believe that.

'Right.' Jobling smiles. 'We won't keep you any longer – get that hot chocolate down you, Azam – but we'll be in touch again next week, or earlier if there's anything to report.' They both drain their mugs.

'You have some impressive hot choccie drinking skills,' Gus says, looking at their empty cups. 'That must have been bare hot fam. And you did it in, like, four mouthfuls.'

'One of the skills you pick up on the job.' Jobling smiles, and they head out of the den and down the hallway.

'So what are we thinking about the new cops on the block?' Hallie asks.

'They seem OK,' I say. 'Better than the last two anyway. But we should still be careful about trusting them.'

'Agreed,' Naira says. 'The list of people we can one hundred per cent trust is scarily short these days.'

We all fall silent again, and I wonder if they're thinking the same thing that I am: that even though we're short on allies, I have more people I trust than I've ever had in my life. 'Cos I have them.

'I've got an early Christmas present for you, Angelo,' Gus says, putting his hot choccie down on the table.

'Is it going to have *Melusine* branding?' I snort while he rummages in his pocket.

'Nah, I'm saving that stuff for actual Christmas.' Gus grins. 'Here you go.' He holds out a badge with a hand-drawn Club Loser logo on it. And this sounds totally stupid but I feel like I might cry.

'Aw, thanks mate,' I say, stuffing it in my pocket because if I look at it for a second longer the tears are going to fall. 'I really appreciate it.'

'I felt like I had to make you one after you went on your death rampage into the killer rats. Bit of an extreme way to prove a point.'

We all laugh because it was such a stupid thing to do, especially without telling the others what was going through my head. I'm lucky they figured it out and that they came to help. Or I'd be dead right now.

'Should have made you one before,' Gus says. 'Genuinely thought you wouldn't want one for some reason.'

'My bad boy persona is obviously working for me,' I grin.

'Nah, we all know you're a nerd.' Colette nudges me.

'Well, didn't they seem great?' Mr C walks in with a massive smile on his face like all his worries have been reassigned like De Salis and Ajao. 'Fellow hot choccie drinkers for the dubs.'

'Probably don't say "for the dubs", sir,' Hallie says.

'Then instead I shall say that they were GOATED.' Mr C grins.

We all groan.

'And talking of the goatiest of GOATS,' Mr C says. 'I have a present for you – something to help you pass the time. Wait here a sec . . .' And he disappears out of the room again.

'Where else are we gonna go?' Hallie yells after him.

'What's this going to be?' I say.

'Probably geography past papers. Or his rock collection.' Colette sighs.

'You couldn't be more wrong!' Mr C comes

back, wheeling a huge, antique-looking machine into the den, a cardboard box balanced on top. 'When you told me about the Songbirds siege, and how you didn't get to enjoy your time there, I had a thought.'

'You're going to have to be more specific, sir, because we have no clue what this is.' Gus stands up to peer into the cardboard box.

'This is a professional karaoke machine that I borrowed from the boyfriend of Mr Morgan's niece who runs karaoke nights at his local pub.' Mr C unravels the cable and plugs it into the wall.

'Mr Morgan the food tech teacher?' Colette asks.

'That's the fella.' Mr Canton nods.

'Random,' Hallie says.

'So I'm going to set this up for you, and then you can sing your cares away. Maybe get in some practice for the school production.' He winks at Naira. 'Singing is very good for the ol' mental health you know.'

'This is actually really great,' Colette says. 'Thank you.'

Mr C smiles around at us all. 'I'm the GOAT, aren't I?'

'Yeah, yeah,' Naira says, pushing past him. 'Give me the mic.'

And we all crack up laughing. Then we sing, and we dance, and we laugh, for hours and hours until Hal's neighbours make a complaint through the video doorbell which makes us laugh even harder. Because even though things are bad, we're still here. Still fighting. Still getting strength from each other and that short list of people that we trust. Club Loser – always better together.

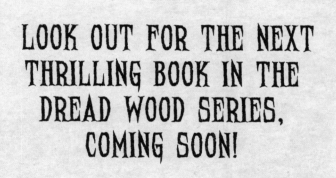

LOOK OUT FOR THE NEXT
THRILLING BOOK IN THE
DREAD WOOD SERIES,
COMING SOON!

FIND OUT WHERE IT ALL BEGAN . . .

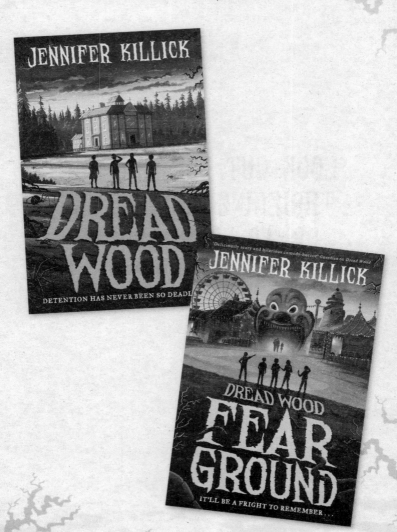

OUT NOW!

THIRTEEN SPOOKY
STORIES TO THRILL,
CHILL AND DELIGHT!

THIRTEEN SPINE-TINGLING TALES

READ,
SCREAM,
REPEAT

CURATED BY

JENNIFER KILLICK

JENNIFER KILLICK

Jennifer Killick is the author of the *Dread Wood* series, *Crater Lake, Crater Lake, Evolution* and the *Alex Sparrow* series. Jennifer regularly visits schools and festivals, and her books have been selected four times for the Reading Agency's Summer Reading Challenge. She lives in Uxbridge, in a house full of children, animals and books. When she isn't busy mothering (which isn't often) she loves to watch scary movies and run as fast as she can, so she is fully prepared for witches, demons, and the zombie apocalypse.